P9-DUZ-425

the
Cool
Cottontail

books by John Ball

the
Cool
Cottontail

by John Ball

Harper & Row, Publishers ～～ New York

acknowledgment

The author would like to express his sincere appreciation to Mrs. Rose Holroyd, Executive Director, and to Mr. Paul Arnold, Director of Public Relations, of the American Sunbathing Association, for invaluable help in the preparation of this book. Similar thanks are also due and tendered to Mr. Carl Apgar, President of the Western Sunbathing Association, and to the managements of Oakdale Ranch, San Bernardino; Olive Dell Ranch, Colton; Glen Eden Sun Club, and the Swallows Club, El Cajon, California.

Grateful acknowledgment is also made to the All-America Karate Federation and in particular to Master Hidetaka Nishiyama for his definitive advice and assistance.

Finally, this book would not have been possible without the generous cooperation of the officers and executives of the Pasadena, California, Police Department, who were unstinting with their time and help.

JOHN BALL

Encino, California
1966

prologue

As the car rolled smoothly along through the night, the man in the back seat found it increasingly difficult to keep his eyes open. He had already been riding for some time, and before that he had had an unusually long and tiring day. At last he gave in and allowed himself the luxury of not caring where he was; he let the many things in his mind come together and overlap one another while he rested his head against the back of the seat. Then, despite the bumps of the road, in a matter of only a minute or two he was sound asleep.

For some time the driver had been watching him very carefully. The low-mounted rear-vision mirror made this simple; a slight shift of position brought the passenger easily into view without his being able to notice it. Presently it became obvious that the tired man was more than just dozing; his mouth was open and his breath made an audible sound as it went in and out with the rise and fall of his chest.

The driver maintained a steady pace for another twenty minutes and then swung off onto a side road slowly enough so that the unfamiliar motion of the turn would not rouse the passenger.

On the narrower road, the driver kept the car's speed even and moderate so that anyone who saw it passing would not take special notice of it. There was almost no other traffic. Twice roads branched off to high and deserted canyons, but the car continued steadily ahead. Then the low-beam headlights picked up a sign and the brake lights came on.

When the car pulled up quietly at the side of the blacktop pavement, it was in a position where the driver could see the loom of the lights of an oncoming vehicle for a considerable distance in either direction. The sleeping man, now slumped in total relaxation, had no idea when the headlights were cut or when the driver gently opened the door next to where he sat.

For a few seconds the driver stared without any emotion at the face of the sleeping man. Then he checked quickly that no cars were coming as far as could be seen in either direction; the night was totally dark and silent. The place was right and the time would never be better. The driver gulped in a deep lungful of air and then struck with vicious, violent power.

The sleeping man slumped a little more and the breath flowed slowly out of his mouth into the still air of the night. He had no sense of pain, no knowledge even that his sleep had been disturbed. When the second smashing blow hit him, he was oblivious to it. His chest no longer moved. The third massive blow smashed two bones in his body, but he was beyond caring. Sometime in the next few seconds he died.

When the last blow, the most vicious of all, struck the man, his body received it, but his spirit was no longer present to be outraged. The driver knew that his victim was already dead, but long and careful training forbade the taking of any unnecessary chances. Making sure could do no harm; not doing so could lead to the gas chamber.

Along the thick shrubbery that lined the road on the south

side, there was a small opening and a turnoff. The driver, after checking once more for intruding headlights, walked ahead to see that by no possible chance anyone was hidden there watching. He found no one. Looking down the narrow half roadway that broke off at the gap, the driver saw only the comforting blackness and, very faintly, the glint of water.

A fresh cadaver, especially of a substantial and solidly built male, is an incredibly awkward and damning possession. The driver was aware of this, but he already knew exactly what he had to do.

The dead man felt no indignation when hands began to undo and pull off his clothing, when fingers were thrust into his mouth and the two carefully made dentures that fitted over his gums were pulled out and thrust into the pocket of his coat. For a moment the person who had done all this contemplated slicing off the tips of the dead man's fingers to destroy any possibility of his prints being taken and identified; then he decided it would not be necessary.

Only the night watched while the murderer rolled the dead man's clothes and possessions into a neat tight bundle and then searched carefully to be sure nothing had fallen out that someone might later be able to identify. Satisfied that the work had been completed, the driver placed the bundle on the front seat of the car, using the open window so that the automatic light would not come on an unnecessary time, and then turned to do one more essential thing.

In five minutes the engine of the car came once more to life and the driver backed cautiously onto the paved road. There was still no evidence of any other traffic, but the rigid necessity to avoid taking chances still held good. Not until the car was safely shielded by the heavy shrubbery did the driver turn on the lights, and then only the low beam. The car departed as it had come, as a carefully chosen pace unlikely to be noticed by anyone. Soon its red tail lights vanished around a turn and the peace of the night returned once more.

x *

the
Cool
Cottontail

chapter 1

Forrest Nunn was awake before the hands of his electric alarm had reached quarter to eight. He pushed down the plunger that would silence the bell and allowed himself a minute or two of total luxury in his warm bed. Then, feeling a little guilty that his wife was up before him, he pushed the bedclothes aside and swung himself to his feet. For a moment he rubbed the palms of his hands across his face to rouse himself further, and then stepped into the bathroom.

At forty-six he did not look his age by a good ten years. His bare body was comfortably on the lean side, well muscled, and deeply tanned. There was no break in its sun-deepened tone below his waist; he was uniformly darkened all over except for the undersides of his arms where the skin color was visibly lighter. He brushed his teeth, shaved, and then stepped under a stinging shower. He was toweling himself when he detected the welcome aroma of frying bacon and caught the sounds of breakfast being prepared in the kitchen of the converted farmhouse.

Quickly he ran a comb through his wet thick hair, pushed his feet into a pair of well-used leather sandals, and, otherwise entirely nude, walked down the hallway toward the kitchen.

He was halfway there when he met his older daughter. She was a buoyant eighteen, at the mid-point between adolescence and womanhood, pretty by any standard and beautiful by some. Her hair, worn loose about her face, set off the wide spacing of her blue eyes, which were her best feature. Her body was near perfection, still that of a girl in outline, but with the depth and symmetry of fast-approaching full maturity. She was wearing nothing, and even in the restricted lighting of the hallway her young skin seemed to glow with a golden-bronze color.

"Morning, Daddy," she said, and smiled at her father.

"Good morning, Linda." He laid his hand on her bare shoulder for a moment; then, together, they went to the kitchen.

It was a very large room at the back of the house, with windows on three of its four sides. The morning sunlight streamed in to burn brilliant patterns on the linoleum and brighten every corner of the clean, well-scrubbed interior, which Forrest had spent long hours rebuilding to make it exactly the way his wife had wanted it to be. The many windows offered a wide view of well-maintained grounds, with the children's playground on the left and the main parking area, which was surrounded by shrubbery, on the right. To the center, concealed by a small grove of trees and the picnic area, were the big pool, volleyball courts and other game facilities, the main sunning lawn, and the beginning of hiking trails that wound up through the foothills of the San Bernardino Mountains.

Emily Nunn, who was actually two years older than her husband, looked even younger than he did and could have passed as being in her early thirties. There was no evidence of middle-age spread in her firm slender body, which was partially concealed by the ample cooking apron she wore tied around a waist as smooth and shapely as her daughter's. Her Swedish descent was revealed by her naturally ash-colored hair.

"Where's George?" Forrest asked after he had come into the room. Before his wife could answer, he reached over and kissed her with gentle tenderness on the cheek.

"He just left to do the main pool," Emily answered. "He wanted to get it finished so he could go into town later this morning. Something about the Little League finals."

"Hank and Mary's son is playing third base for the Tigers," Linda added. "That makes four nudists in the series—two of ours, one from Glen Eden, and one from Olive Dell."

As she finished, there was the sound of running bare feet and nine-year-old Carole erupted through the doorway. "I'm going to the game with George," she announced without stopping. She hurried to the breakfast table and popped into her chair in a single continuous motion.

"Did you brush your teeth?" Forrest asked his younger daughter.

She looked at him and curled her lips in disappointment. "All right," she said slowly, and raised her slight body from the wooden chair. As she turned to go, her father gave her a playful slap on her bare buttocks for a reminder.

"Teeth and hair brushed, and hands and face thoroughly washed," he admonished. "No breakfast until you do—ever."

With the appearance of utter weariness that a frustrated child can summon at an instant's notice, Carole plodded back across the room and disappeared into the living quarters of the house.

Forrest turned again to his wife. "If the lumber gets here in time, I plan to spend most of the day on the sauna. There's a couple with three children coming for an interview about eleven. Will you handle it for me?"

"Should I dress?" Linda asked.

Forrest nodded. "I think so; they have a sixteen-year-old son and this will be their first visit. Don't put on a sun robe. I don't want him to break his neck trying to look around corners."

Linda smiled at him. "I know better than that. We'll take care of them."

As Emily Nunn turned back toward the range where she was preparing breakfast, her attention was caught by her son George, whom she saw emerging from the grove of trees that screened the pool area. When he started to run across the grass toward the house, she knew instantly that something was wrong. It did not need to be anything serious, but she looked quickly at her husband and silently flashed him a message.

Forrest Nunn read it correctly but did not allow himself to be unduly disturbed. George was twenty-four, but there was still a good deal of boy in him yet, and a clogged filter in the pool was about the worst to be expected.

When George came in through the outside doorway, Forrest looked at him and immediately changed his opinion. His son's face had a mature set, with unusual tightness at the corners of his mouth. Something as minor as a mechanical problem would not cause him to look like that.

The young man crossed the room and spoke softly to his father. "Dad, can I see you for a moment?" There was urgency in his voice.

Forrest nodded and followed his son into the outside sunlight. As soon as the door had closed behind them, George turned. "Dad, there was a dead man, nude, floating in the main pool. I just pulled him out."

"Who is it?" Forrest asked quickly.

"I don't know him. Man of about fifty or so, floating face down. I got him out and thought of artificial respiration, but he was gone—cold as ice."

"Go back and try to revive him anyway. You know what to do. Keep at it—he may still be alive no matter how he feels. I'll join you as soon at I call the sheriff."

George turned and ran back toward the trees and the pool. Almost as rapidly Forrest returned to the kitchen, threw a quick "It's all right" to his wife, and went to the telephone. He glanced at the emergency-number list posted on the wall and then dialed swiftly. When he heard the ringing on the other end of the line, he consciously relaxed so that his voice would be normal when he spoke. "This is Forrest Nunn at Sun Valley Lodge. My son has just discovered a nude body floating in our main pool."

"I can't say I'm surprised," the voice on the line commented.

"I didn't make myself clear; this isn't one of our people. I haven't seen him yet, but according to my son he is a stranger. He's being given artificial respiration, but George is sure that he's dead."

The voice at the other end became crisper. "Keep up the respiration until we get there. Mouth-to-mouth, if possible. Try not to disturb the area any more than is necessary. We'll come as soon as we can."

The line went dead.

Forrest returned at once to the kitchen to face his wide-eyed, worried wife and their two daughters. "Carole," he directed, "I want you to go to your room and stay there until I call you. You're a good girl and you aren't being punished. Run!"

Carole looked very disappointed but nevertheless obeyed immediately.

When she was safely beyond hearing, Forrest said calmly, "George has found a man, a stranger, floating in our pool. He thinks the man is dead, but he's applying artificial respiration anyway. I've sent for the sheriff's rescue squad. Please stay away from the pool area and see that no one else goes there. Linda, dress and put the chain up on the gate. Don't let anybody in, not even our members, until the sheriff's squad arrives; then take your orders from whoever is in charge."

"How about the new couple?" Linda asked quickly.

"If they come in the meantime, have them use the private driveway and offer them some coffee. If you have to, explain we have had something unusual occur and will be with them as soon as we can."

Linda nodded her understanding and hurried after her sister.

"Is that all?" Emily asked.

"So far, yes. I'm going down to the pool to spell George. Handle things, will you?"

Emily nodded. "If you need me, call."

Forrest reached for a pair of sun-bleached khaki shorts where they lay conveniently ready, picked up another pair for his son, and left. Emily watched him as he crossed the lawn with long swift strides and disappeared down the pathway through the grove that led to the pool area on the other side.

chapter 2

Along the stretch of public road that bordered the grounds of Sun Valley Lodge, there was a solid screen of shrubbery and trees unbroken except for the main entrance driveway and a smaller road some distance away for the private use of the owners. Opposite the principal gateway there was a sign, which read:

SUN VALLEY LODGE
Affiliated with the A.S.A. and W.S.A.
Visitors Welcome
(Please use gate phone)

Even though the public road was only a two-lane macadam-topped secondary highway, the thin stream of traffic it carried added up to a surprisingly large number of cars by the end of the long California summer. The road followed the foothills for some miles and then turned up toward the mountains and the high resort area, where it joined the main routes to Big Bear Lake and the winter ski sites. By taking a branch, the knowledgeable driver could end up at the El Cajon pass and cut many miles off the established through-way route from Los Angeles across the desert to Las Vegas.

Of the sum total of cars which traveled the relatively obscure cutoff route past the lodge, a few turned in. Many other drivers who glanced at the sign in passing weren't even aware that the abbreviations represented the American Sunbathing Association and its regional subdivision, the Western Sunbathing Association.

Linda Nunn knew every part of the lodge grounds and every foot of its hiking trails; she had lived there since she was ten years old. As soon as she saw her father take off toward the sheltering trees that guarded the big pool, she hurried to her room wondering how any stranger, dead or alive, could have got to the carefully protected recreation area without having been seen from the house. Buried in the entrance driveway, there was a concealed treadle that rang a bell in both the office and the kitchen whenever a car drove in; the warning device had not rung the night before.

Opening her closet door, Linda snatched a dress from a hanger and slipped it over her head. She did not bother with underwear; she was not planning to leave the park grounds and expected soon to be free of clothing again, possibly within the hour. Though her closet and dresser were full of the usual things found in a young lady's wardrobe, wearing any more than was absolutely necessary at the lodge was pointless. The dress she had chosen was conservatively cut and would do nicely.

She paused for a brief moment at her mirror and gave her hair a pat or two before she hurried out of the room. Her feet in attractive and well-made sandals felt the springiness of thick Bermuda grass as she walked rapidly across the big front lawn, taking the short cut to the members' entrance. She arrived slightly out of breath, but in time to put up the chain that had been provided against any circumstance which might require that the grounds be temporarily closed. With this done she paused to collect herself and speculate on what would be likely to happen next.

Eight minutes later she heard the distant high whine of a siren. It was not continuous, but sounded only now and then as the approaching vehicle hit curves in the road where a warning was necessary. She had heard that same pattern many times before, even in that quiet rural area. This time, she knew, the emergency equipment was coming to her home and the realization gave her a strange and uncomfortable feeling.

The sound grew louder until she could distinguish that there were two cars, one close behind the other. With a final blast from the sirens the vehicles came into view, a copper-colored patrol car closely followed by a police ambulance with the word "RESCUE" visible on its side. The lead driver, who obviously knew exactly where the lodge driveway was, pulled up and stopped.

When he leaned out to speak, he was crisp but pleasant. "Is there a service road down to your pool?" he asked.

Linda hesitated a moment. "Yes, but we don't use it very often. It's pretty rutty."

"That's all right. Which way do we go?"

"You have to use the other driveway. Shall I show you?"

"Please."

Because there were two men in the front seat of the car, Linda opened the rear door and climbed in. Sitting on the edge of the seat, she directed the driver to the other entryway, down past the onetime farmhouse, and onto the dirt road that skirted the edge of the trees. The sheriff's car bumped heavily over exposed tree roots and soft sandy potholes for a hundred yards and then drew up beside a complicated filter system that serviced a beautifully decked Olympic-size swimming pool.

When Linda reached to open the door, she discovered there were no handles on the inside of the car. The man beside the driver let her out and followed as she led the way up an embankment to the deck level. The smooth surface of the water stole a deep blue from the sky and created a false feeling of calm serenity. Midway up the side of the elaborate concrete decking, George Nunn was lying prone, face to face with the body of a substantially built man, stark nude in the strong light of the sun. George, with his fingers around his lips, was doing his best to force mouth-to-mouth air into the lungs of the inert man. Forrest was kneeling beside his son, watching for any sign of reviving life.

After a quick glance at the scene, the sheriff's deputy next to Linda reached for her shoulder and turned her away. "You'd better leave us now, Miss," he advised.

"I've seen dead people before," she answered quickly. "That is, if he's really dead." She looked back and saw that two more men were getting out of the ambulance, which had followed them down the road.

The deputy took a firmer tone. "He's not covered, Miss."

Linda looked at him. "I'm not a cottontail," she retorted. "And I might know him. I know everyone who comes here and a good many other members, too."

While they were talking, a surprisingly young-looking man carrying a doctor's familiar black kit brushed past and knelt beside the man on the deck. He motioned George away and laid his ear against the man's chest. A moment later he rolled up an eyelid and then listened carefully with a stethoscope on the side of the chest next to the left arm. He shook his head. Experimentally he flexed the arm itself and then rose to his feet. "He's gone," he announced. "Probably several hours ago."

He looked at George. "You did exactly the right thing in trying to revive him. If you'd been in time, you might have saved him." He turned. "Get the girl out of here," he ordered.

"She's my daughter," Forrest said mildly. "She's seen death before."

The young doctor opened his mouth, remembered where he was, and closed it again. "At least let's cover him up," he said finally.

The ambulance driver brought a blanket and laid it over the body.

The senior deputy was an older man; his body was thick around his middle, where much of his weight had settled, making him look shorter than he was. He appeared in his early fifties, but added five years more when he took off his uniform cap to wipe his arm across his forehead. His hair had turned largely white, and over much of the top where his cap had rested it was gone altogether. When he had wiped the perspiration away, he replaced his cap, produced a small notebook, and asked calmly, "What happened?"

George answered. "I came down not much more than half an hour ago to clean the tiling and backwash the filters—we do it every other day. When I came through the trees"—he stopped and pointed—"I saw him floating in the pool. He was back up, with his face in the water. I was surprised because I hadn't heard any guests come in and early Tuesday morning isn't a usual time for the pool to be in use. When he didn't pull his face out of the water after half a minute or so, I knew something was wrong. I ran the rest of the way and dove in. I pulled him out and put him on the deck where he is now.

I was pretty sure he was dead—he was cold—then I ran for Dad."

"If you dove in after him, how come your shorts aren't wet?" the deputy asked.

"I didn't have them on at the time."

"Do you know this man?"

George shook his head. "I don't and Dad doesn't. He isn't a member here, that's for sure."

"I don't think he's a member anywhere," Linda contributed unexpectedly. "Maybe a onetime visitor, or an occasional who goes to one of the northern clubs, but no more than that."

The deputy turned and looked at her. "I'm sure you have a reason for saying that," he prompted. "Would you mind telling me?"

"He's a cottontail," Linda pointed out. "He isn't tanned at all around the hips, you could see that clearly. He couldn't be a nudist and have skin that white anywhere."

The deputy wrote in his notebook, then looked down at the doctor, who had resumed his examination of the body. "What do you think?" he asked.

The doctor got to his feet after replacing the covering. "I don't think he drowned. Possibly an accident, but more likely he was murdered."

The senior deputy nodded. "About what I figured. He doesn't appear to belong here. And if he had come in for a midnight swim without the owner's consent, he would have some sort of a vehicle. He could have walked in, but if he did, where are his clothes?"

He turned to the driver who had accompanied him. "Call in and tell them what we have," he directed. "Ask if Virgil is still there. If he is, maybe it would be a good idea if he stopped by."

The other man nodded and returned to his patrol car. In little more than a minute he was back with a report. "Virgil was just walking out the door, but they caught him. He said he'd look in on his way back to Pasadena. They're going to call Chief Addis and ask if we can have him if it works out we need him. He asked to have the body left where it is until he gets here."

"Will that be long?" Forrest asked.

"I don't think so," the senior deputy answered. "He doesn't know this area the way we do, but he should be here inside a half hour."

"Meanwhile, then, come up to the house and have some coffee. It's ready—it always is." He motioned toward the pathway.

"Somebody will have to stay with the body."

The ambulance driver, who had remained silently in the background, raised his right hand shoulder high to volunteer and sank into one of the aluminum deck chairs. Forrest led the rest of the small party through the grove and toward the residence on the other side. Linda fell in beside the man in charge, whose uniform already showed dark marks of perspiration under the armpits.

"Who's Virgil?" she asked.

The deputy looked at her a moment before he replied. "In Virgil's case it might be best to wait until you meet him. Then you'll know."

chapter 3

Forrest Nunn held the door open to the big bright kitchen, where his wife, who had seen them coming, was already setting out the coffee cups. It was characteristic of her that she counted her guests first and then took time to wonder what was going on. "Please sit down, gentlemen," she invited. "The coffee is ready and I'll have sweet rolls for you in a moment."

The deputy in charge, who was at once fully aware that his hostess was wearing a coverall type of apron and nothing more, regarded it as one more curiosity in the line of duty and took it in his stride. "Bill Morrissey, ma'am," he introduced himself. A little gingerly he walked past her and stood waiting at the table. The other deputy, who was much younger and considerably less self-possessed, mumbled his name and hurried to join his partner, his eyes toward the floor. The back of his neck was red and he shifted his weight slightly from one foot to the other.

The young doctor was close to being rude. He introduced himself then stood stiffly to one side. Emily Nunn realized immediately that he wanted her to see his disapproval, and just as quickly decided to let him stew. It was doubtful if he had turned thirty yet. She noted that and thought he had a good deal to learn about people before he could be a real success in his profession.

"Please sit down." She indicated the waiting table. "Linda, will you serve the rolls while I pour the coffee?"

Forrest took his place at the head of the table and motioned Morrissey to a chair beside him. The deputy eased himself down slowly with the air of a man who can fit himself in anywhere. The other deputy took his chair nervously and, for something to do, looked carefully into his empty coffee cup apparently to see if it was clean. It was.

Emily picked up an oversize electric percolator and, beginning with the senior deputy, filled the cups. She poured one at a vacant place and, turning brightly to the doctor, asked, "Do you take cream, sugar, or both?"

"Black," the doctor answered tersely. It was a moment before he realized he had been trapped; since he had specified how he would like his coffee, he would now have to drink it. With the corners of his mouth held tight he came to the table and reluctantly sat down. Linda did not ask if he would like one of the freshly baked rolls; she put one on his plate.

As Emily turned to set the large percolator on the table within easy reach of everyone, Bill Morrissey reconfirmed that the big apron she was wearing did not reach completely around her body. He picked up a spoon and stirred his coffee.

Forrest broke his roll and asked Morrissey for the butter. "During the summer we have a lot of your people in and out of the park," he commented. "Joe Thompson, Mike Marino, Ed Meyers, but I think this is the first time you've been here."

"That's right," Morrissey admitted easily. "I usually stay at the station and answer the complaints. Heard a lot about your place, of course." He sipped his coffee and made a small decision. "About the only resort around here where we've never had a squawk."

"That's nice to hear," Forrest acknowledged. "We don't have a bar, of course, and that has its benefits. Also we're pretty selective about our membership."

Emily, her guests served, sat down at the end of the table and motioned her daughter to sit beside her. "Have you ever been in a nudist park before, doctor?" she asked pleasantly.

"No, I have not." He bit the words off at the edge of courtesy.

"We get a lot of our people through medical advice, you know. It's too bad you're not married; otherwise we'd like to have you and your wife come out for the weekend as our guests."

The doctor looked at her clinically. "How do you know about me?" he asked.

Emily smiled. "Single men are quite easy to spot—at least we find it so. Let me warm your coffee."

As the doctor drew breath to decline, the gate phone rang. Linda rose quickly to answer it.

"This is Mr. Tibbs," the voice on the line said. "I took the liberty of walking in past your chain to use the phone. This is the nudist camp, I believe?"

"This is the nudist resort," Linda corrected. "Are you a member of any other nudist organization, here or abroad?"

"No, I'm not."

"Are you married, sir?"

"No, not yet. I still have hopes."

"I'll be right out." Linda hung up the phone. "Another

16   *

single," she reported to her father. "Is *he* behind the times! He called this a nudist *camp*."

"At least he didn't call it a colony," Emily said gently.

"Well, he's a cottontail at any rate. I'll go take care of him."

"Did he give his name?" Deputy Morrissey asked.

"Tibbs," Linda said.

"Now that I know what that word means, I can tell you he isn't a cottontail."

Linda looked at him for a moment, waiting for him to go on. When he gave no sign of further comment, she shrugged her shoulders slightly and confidently went out the door. As she started across the big lawn for the second time that morning, she recalled how many single men had applied at the gate, some of them very nice, others clearly not. Worst of all were the occasional cars filled with four or five men, all professing interest, all carrying cameras, and all with families that had been carefully left behind. But she had handled many would-be sightseers, and none of them frightened her. When she went to meet people at the gate, she knew that if she did not reappear or call in within five minutes, her father would be out immediately, to take over if need be.

When she reached the entrance, there was a plain black Ford sedan pulled up in front of the chain; standing beside it, a man was waiting.

Linda saw many things quickly. She saw that he was probably in his early thirties, that he was of medium height, rather slender, and dressed in a quiet business suit. But these were secondary impressions. The thing that she saw first, and which overshadowed everything else, was the fact that he was a Negro.

For an instant her confidence fled; she had never met a Negro applicant at the gate before, and she had no Negro friends. As a rule, if a single man presented himself unintroduced, she would automatically and courteously turn him away; it was the lodge policy. But if she did that now, the man might think it was because of his race, which wouldn't be true.

Without knowing how, she sensed that he understood her embarrassment. He came forward a few steps and then stopped, meeting her halfway.

"My name is Virgil Tibbs," he said. "The sheriff's office asked me to stop by. I'm a police officer."

Linda's first sensation was relief—she would not have to turn him away. So this was Virgil! At that moment she remembered Deputy Morrissey's remark that he was not a cottontail. Morrissey had been right; the joke was on her. As she unhooked the chain, she made up her mind that in a nice way she would get even with Morrissey. He could have told her what to expect.

"Come in, Mr. Tibbs," she invited. "You understand that this is a nudist park. The parking lot for visitors is right ahead. Leave your car and follow the path to the lodge. I'll meet you there."

"Thank you," Tibbs said. He got back into his car without further comment and drove in. As she replaced the chain, Linda thought that his voice was a nice one, moderate and controlled, and without any trace of an accent. She took the short cut across the grass once more and waited a hundred feet from the main building. She wanted to see how Tibbs would walk; she could tell a lot about people by the way they carried themselves, particularly when they were entering nudist premises for the first time. As she stood there, the sounds of singing birds filled her ears and the air was rich with the sense of life and of growing things. It was difficult to remember that in the midst of all this a dead man lay down on the pool deck covered with a blanket. A man who might have been murdered.

When Virgil Tibbs joined her, she approved his walk as good. She felt that he had confidence—not the aggressive kind, but the bearing of a man who knows his way. It was also a quiet kind of confidence, the sort you have to look for to see.

The birds continued to declare that God was in his heaven and all was right with the world.

"The others are in the kitchen having coffee," Linda explained. "Would you like to join them there?"

"It might be better if you showed me—where the trouble is," Tibbs answered.

"This way." She liked the fact that he put business first; her father had taught her the importance of that.

When they came out of the grove, she discovered that the deputies and the doctor had returned to the pool area. She had a quick odd reaction—they had done that so Tibbs would find them on the job. That made him something more, perhaps, than just a regular policeman.

"Are you a detective?" she asked.

"The Pasadena police call me an investigator," he answered.

"An investigator is a detective, isn't he?"

Tibbs looked at her and smiled a little grimly. "He'd better be if he wants to keep his job," he replied. In a few more steps they reached the pool deck.

After nodding to the men, Tibbs lifted a corner of the

blanket, glanced at the body, and walked back a few steps to where Linda was standing. "Thank you for bringing me down here," he said. He stopped at that point, knowing that she would understand he wanted her to leave.

Linda looked at him steadily. "The body is nude. I've already seen it. I'm not going to faint or act up just because he's dead."

Tibbs returned her look just as steadily. "If you were me," he asked, "how would you feel about taking the covering off the dead body of a naked man in front of an attractive young lady?"

Without looking Linda sensed that Bill Morrissey was standing a few paces away watching and listening.

"That would depend on the young lady," she answered. "Any young lady, I wouldn't do it. But suppose that the young lady in question had lived eight years in a nudist park and looked on anatomy the way you look on a pair of shoes. Suppose she had thought of going to medical school. And suppose she wanted to learn whatever she could whenever she could. What then?"

Tibbs pressed his lips together and the corners of his mouth quirked. Then Linda followed him as he walked back toward the corpse, and she stood six feet behind him when the cover was removed. Despite her confident statement, she wondered just how she was going to feel, not knowing what they were going to do. She decided to keep her mind focused on watching the investigation and to keep all other ideas out of her head. It would be interesting to see how much she could notice and detect on her own.

She guessed the man's age as fifty. His hair was well and recently cut; that probably meant he had not been living away in the woods someplace. His face was full, clean-shaven, and, despite the look of death, she felt that he had probably been a nice man. If he had applied at the gate with his family, she would have passed him as far as the parking lot and called her father. She had a quick idea and looked at his nails. They were clean and well cut—didn't look like a workman's hands. He had been an executive—something like that.

She studied the white marks where he had worn bathing trunks; they had been briefs and to her practiced eye it was clear he had seldom if ever been out of doors without them at least. There was a scar on his body where he had had his appendix removed. She also made careful note of one additional fact.

The Negro detective was on his knees beside the body, his fingers pressing the cold flesh here and there, and once he opened the jaws and looked into the dead man's mouth. Linda admitted to herself she would not like to do that. The thought of medical school, which had been a hazy one at best, retreated further in her mind.

Tibbs got to his feet. "You can take him away now," he said to the ambulance driver. "I don't know yet whether I'm going to be officially assigned to this or not. If I am, then I'll want the lab and P.M. reports."

The driver went down the short embankment to his vehicle and returned with a long wicker basket. As Linda moved back to allow more room, the driver and the junior deputy placed the body in the carrier. The body was heavy and Tibbs gave them a hand.

"Do you need us any more?" Morrissey asked.

"No, go ahead," Tibbs answered. "I'll look around a bit and wait for orders. Have them call me at the resort office." He turned to Linda. "Is your phone listed?" he asked.

"Of course. We have an ad in the yellow pages." She supplied the number.

When the vehicles had gone, she remembered to offer the usual hospitality. "Come up and have a cup of coffee," she suggested. "You can meet the rest of the family."

"I'd like to do that," he answered. "But I want to look around here a little first. Are you expecting any guests today?"

"We don't have any specific reservations, but some people will probably show up. Perhaps quite a few."

Tibbs looked up into the sky in the general direction of the sun. "Would you mind if I took off my coat?" he inquired.

"Here?" Linda retorted. "Well, what do you think! By all means. Put your clothes on one of the chairs and be comfortable. And use the pool, too, if you don't mind the fact there was a body in it. The showers are right there." She pointed.

In a moment she sensed his embarrassment and misread it. "Don't tell me you're worried about my being here—" she began.

Tibbs managed to interrupt her. "I said 'coat.' We have rules in the police department."

"We have rules here, too," Linda countered. "You're an exception because you're here on business."

Tibbs took off his coat and hung it across the back of one of the chairs.

"Tie," Linda said. "Compromise."

"Do you promise to stop there?"

Linda giggled. "I promise."

Tibbs undid his tie and laid it carefully over his coat. He

was wearing a short-sleeved white shirt; when he opened the neck, Linda thought he looked quite handsome. "Now aren't you more comfortable?" she asked.

"I certainly am," Tibbs admitted.

"See?"

Tibbs smiled. "Don't waste your time in medical school; study law and develop your natural talents."

"How about becoming a policewoman?" Linda asked.

Tibbs looked at her carefully. "All right, let's say you are a policewoman. You know this area, and against my better judgment you have seen the body. Now, what are your deductions?"

Linda drew breath and gathered her thoughts. When she spoke, it was as though she were delivering a formal report. "The victim was a man approximately fifty years of age. He was not a laboring man—probably an executive. He took pride in his appearance—at least he was careful about it. I would say that he was neat in his habits. He wasn't a nudist. On the whole, I would say that he was a nice man." She paused and looked at the Negro detective. "How did I do?"

"Not badly," he admitted. "You saw quite a few things. I had a closer look than you did, and have considerably more experience."

"How much experience? Have you worked on murders before?"

Tibbs answered her patiently, "I've been a policeman more than ten years. Yes, I've worked on murders. I'm something of a specialist in crimes against persons—things like murder, extortion, assault with deadly weapons, armed robbery—"

"And, of course, rape."

"Young lady—" Tibbs began.

"What did I miss? About the body, I mean," Linda interjected quickly.

Tibbs sat down on a concrete pool bench and locked his fingers together. "Well," he began, "you saw the haircut, the fingernails, and the bathing-trunk marks. For a first try I'd say that was good."

"He had had his appendix out, too," Linda added.

"Good. That's a sound point of information. Doing a little guessing, I would add these facts: the victim, as you call him, had probably been living abroad and only recently came to this country. He may have spoken with an accent. There is a good chance that he was an excellent swimmer. I think I would disagree with you that he was an executive; it seems more probable that he had independent means or possibly a person who worked only occasionally. Considering his age, it would be fairly possible that he was retired. For a real long shot, I would hazard a guess as to his profession. I'd say he was an unusually good technical man of some sort—perhaps an engineer."

Linda stood and looked at him. "I'm impressed," she said.

"You shouldn't be. Go back to your Sherlock Holmes and reread *A Study in Scarlet*. See what the head of this business did with an empty room in a deserted house and part of a word written on the wall. A whole word," he corrected.

"I'm still impressed. I see why you're a detective."

Tibbs shook his head. "You certainly saw several good points, but you missed a very big one."

"Well, I did hold out on you a little," Linda confessed. "I don't know you very well yet, but I know something about that man's religion. I'm pretty sure he was a gentile, at least I'm certain he wasn't orthodox."

Tibbs looked at her. "You *are* a most remarkable young lady," he conceded. "I held out on you, too, and I'm very glad that I did."

"Tell me," Linda said anxiously. "I gave you all I had."

Tibbs shook his head. "I'm sorry, I can't do that. But suppose you put together all the facts you now have and see if you can add them up into something."

Linda thought. "The motive was robbery," she suggested. "They took everything he had, even his clothes."

Tibbs pressed his fingers together hard. "That was minor to the real crime; they took his *life*—almost the worst thing there is."

"What is the worst?"

"Treason. But you're still overlooking the important thing."

"Please tell me."

"Put together the basic facts: here is a body found entirely without clothing or jewelry, granted that you're used to things like that around here—being without clothing, I mean. However, you said yourself he wasn't a nudist. He had full upper and lower dentures and they, too, have been removed. He was brought here sometime during the night without arousing your family and dumped into your pool. Why?"

"To embarrass us, to damage the nudist idea."

"I hardly think so. Don't you see, young lady, he was left like that in a strange place where he obviously didn't belong, even without his teeth—"

Linda opened her mouth and drew a quick breath. "So that no one would know who he was!"

"We can identify him, but it may take time, valuable time."

"May I ask something?"

"Go ahead."

"If the murderer wanted to make identification difficult, or even impossible, why did he leave the body here where we would be sure to find it right away? There are hundreds of places right near here where he could have rolled it off a cliff and maybe no one would have found it for weeks. Some of the canyon roads go through pretty wild country."

Tibbs looked at his locked fingers and then at her. "Now you're beginning to get somewhere. At the moment I don't know the answer to that question. For the time being, at least, it's the crux of the problem."

chapter 4

Forrest Nunn emerged from the grove of trees in a clearly disturbed frame of mind. As he approached the pool and saw Tibbs for the first time, his face betrayed a shadow of surprise, but he controlled himself well. "Are you Mr. Tibbs?" he asked.

"Yes, I am." The Negro detective offered his hand; he did not thrust it out, but made the gesture quietly. Forrest took it.

"I'm sorry I couldn't get here sooner; I was on the phone," he explained. "The paper called. We have some good friends down there and I couldn't cut them off even though I know very little about what's been happening."

He turned to his daughter. "Linda, I suspect that you may be in the way here. Perhaps I am, too." He looked at Tibbs.

"You must be Mr. Nunn," Tibbs said. "And this, I take it, is your daughter. We have been conferring on the case."

"I'm sorry," Forrest apologized. He introduced himself and Linda, then dispatched his daughter back to the lodge building. "I hope she didn't annoy you," he said. "She's at the curious age when she wants to know all about everything and considers herself quite an adult. In a way she is, but in a good many other respects she's still a young girl."

Tibbs nodded. "I'd like to look around for an hour or so

if you don't mind. Then I may want to ask some questions."

"Take your time," Forrest replied. "I'll keep everyone else away from here for as long as you like. When you've finished, come up to the house and we'll talk."

"Fine," Tibbs agreed.

For almost an hour and a half he made a detailed examination of every part of the pool area, the deck, and the access road. When finally he returned to the place where he had left his coat and tie, he was intercepted by a small well-browned girl who appeared from the pathway through the trees.

"You're Mr. Tibbs," she announced. "Do you know who I am?"

"You're a jaybird," Tibbs suggested.

"No, I'm Carole. My daddy sent me with a message. Mr. Addis called you."

"Chief Addis?" Tibbs asked quickly.

"Well, not exactly." She consulted a slip of paper in her hand. "It was Mr. Harnois. Do you know him?"

"Larry Harnois? I certainly do. He's a police officer in Pasadena. So am I. What did Mr. Harnois say?"

Carole drew breath and accepted her moment of importance. "He said to tell you that Chief Addis wants you to help the people here and find out who killed the man in our pool. Where is he?" She looked quickly around.

"Some of my friends took him away in an ambulance," Tibbs answered.

"Oh." Carole was disappointed.

Carefully Tibbs slipped his tie under his collar and knotted it.

"Why did you do that?" Carole asked.

"So that I will look nice," Tibbs answered. "At least as nice as I can."

"I liked you better the other way."

He laughed and looked at her. "Is Linda your sister?" he asked.

"Yes."

"Are there any more sisters?"

"No."

"That's good," Tibbs said a little grimly.

Carole studied him. "We have a very nice mommy," she volunteered.

"I'm sure of that. Now I have to talk to your father. Would you like to show me the way?"

Emily Nunn had dressed in a sleeveless yellow Capri outfit, as she expected there would be a deluge of policemen in and out most of the day. Whenever non-nudist visitors were expected at the lodge, she dressed as a matter of principle, though if they came unexpectedly, she felt that since they knew they were in a nudist park any problems of conforming were up to them.

Virgil Tibbs' first impression of her when he followed Carole into the kitchen was of a moderately tall, astonishingly youthful-looking woman, and one completely in possession of herself.

"Good morning, Mr. Tibbs," she greeted him. "I do hope Linda didn't annoy you too much this morning. I was quite upset when I learned she had insisted on staying down there with you."

"Not at all, Mrs. Nunn," Tibbs answered politely. "She's a very interesting young lady. And Carole, too, of course."

"How nice of you to say so." Without asking she set a place for him and poured out a cup of coffee. "I know you want to talk to Forrest—he'll be right down." As she spoke, her husband appeared in the doorway.

For the better part of an hour Tibbs questioned them carefully about the night before, about the usual procedures for gaining access to the lodge grounds, about other possible methods of entry, and about the attitudes of the surrounding community concerning the nudist resort. Linda's suggestion that the body had been put into the pool either as a gruesome prank or to embarrass the park had also occurred to him and he gave it careful attention. In his own mind he doubted it, but that didn't rule it out.

"There are, of course, a good many people who don't like the nudist idea simply because it's different," Forrest told him candidly. "They don't trouble us much. Our community relations are very good and I'm at a loss to suggest anyone who would do such a thing to us. It's pretty hard to imagine that someone would steal a body just to plant it on our property."

"Frankly, I can't see that either. My present thinking is that the body was put into your pool for some entirely different reason."

"I sincerely hope so," Forrest said.

Tibbs also drew a complete blank on identification of the dead man by anyone at the lodge. Emily had not seen the body, but Forrest, Linda, and George all swore they had never seen the man before and would have remembered him if they had. They could offer no suggestion about who he might have been.

Finally Tibbs closed his notebook and said, "I understand that I'm being assigned to this case and will be following it up.

That means I may have to bother you people several times more before it is finished. At the moment I can't think of any reason why, but it usually works out that way."

Forrest nodded. "We understand. Come any time you wish and bring anyone with you you might need. We're almost always here."

Tibbs rose. "Then I believe that's all for the moment. Let me caution you—if you find anything, anything at all, around the grounds that doesn't belong there or that might possibly have a bearing on this matter, please call me immediately." He laid a calling card on the table.

At that moment the warning bell rang indicating that a car had entered the driveway. Tibbs glanced at the clock. It was ten minutes to eleven.

Linda got quickly to her feet. "They must have taken the chain down," she remarked, and disappeared out the doorway.

"If you have no objection, we're going to do a clean-up job on the pool," Forrest said. "I know the body didn't contaminate the water, but some of our members might be disturbed by the idea. I'm going to drain the pool, wash it down, and clean the deck." He followed Tibbs out the doorway.

"Go ahead, do whatever you consider necessary."

As the two men went slowly toward the parking lot, the beauty of the day completely denied the thing that had been discovered that morning. Walking along the sun-bright grass, they met Linda escorting a middle-aged couple, a teen-aged son, and two younger daughters. Tibbs detoured just enough to avoid the need for introductions. When he was well past, the man in Linda's party stopped and turned.

"I guess they don't care who they let in here," he declared with offensive loudness in his voice.

"I'm sorry," Forrest said quietly.

"I'm afraid I may have cost you some business," Tibbs countered. "When you go back, please explain that I'm not a member. Tell them the county sent me to inspect the swimming pool."

Forrest shook his head. "I don't think I will. Along with known Communists, people with abnormal sex ideas, and troublemakers generally, we won't take bigots. Too many of our members are Jewish or Nisei."

They reached the parking lot and Tibbs climbed behind the wheel of his car. "I'll keep you posted as much as I can," he said. "Be sure and call me immediately if anything breaks here."

"I will," Forrest promised.

Tibbs swung his car out the driveway and turned toward San Bernardino. He reported in at the sheriff's station, took care of some preliminary business, and then stopped at the morgue. He had a few words with the attendant in charge, who looked somewhat surprised and disappeared for a few minutes. When he returned, he handed Tibbs a small box of the kind that is commonly used for dispensing pills. After leaving two or three questions for the medical examiner, the Pasadena detective got back into his car once more and, choosing Highway 66 rather than the freeway, drove the seventy-odd miles back to his office.

Upon arrival he parked his car in an assigned slot and made his way to his modest office. It was a bare functional area that he shared with another investigator, but he had worked hard to earn it. He seated himself behind his badly scarred desk, put the little box on top where he could look at it, and leaned back to think.

When he had first joined the Pasadena police, and had completed the training courses set out for him, he had graduated to a uniform and the job of standing most of the day in the broiling sun directing traffic. Later he had been given a three-wheeler to ride, which carried with it the job of going up one street and down another, endlessly, day after day, checking cars for overtime parking. He had patrolled the parking areas during the Rose Bowl game and still remembered the massive roars of the crowd which signified to those outside that some moment of exciting action was in progress.

For six years he patiently performed his basic police tasks while at the same time he occupied a good part of his spare time in another activity. When he was in college, he had become interested in the basic Oriental martial arts: judo, kendo, aikido, and karate. Kendo swordsmanship, while it appealed to him, was of less immediate concern than the arts that he might be able to use in the work he was hoping to do. Gradually his interest had concentrated on the subtle power of aikido and, in almost direct contrast, the Spartan lethal discipline of karate.

In both the schools he had chosen to attend, he had learned to sit erect on his bare feet on the floor, look straight ahead, and address the man in charge as *sensei*. In the aikido *dojo*, on the unyielding tatami mats that offered little comfort, he had learned to fall, to roll, and to deal with opponents with the motions of his hips and wrists. At the karate school, where each session was a test of his muscular control and stamina, he learned to concentrate the entire power of his body with whip-like force. He learned to punch, to kick, to chop, to strike, and to thrust, all with lightning speed and total accuracy. He learned to use the edges of his hands, his elbows, his knees, the many parts of his feet that made effective weapons, and to protect himself from similar attacks by possible future opponents.

At these schools none of his teachers ever seemed to notice that he was a Negro. And he had long since dismissed any awareness that some of his teachers and fellow students were Japanese and others were not. In karate sparring, in particular, there was no time for such considerations. An opponent was a man of a certain physical structure and skill; overcoming him, if possible, took total concentration, total dedication to the art of karate, with no possible room for any other thoughts.

In aikido, which he had started relatively late, he wore the brown belt of the *nikyu*.

He had been a policeman for six years, and a dedicated karate student for eight, when a decision concerning him had been made behind the stony faces of the ranked karate examiners. After evaluating him many, many times they at last found him up to a stratospheric standard from which no exceptions were ever made. It had been the proudest, and most humbling, moment of his life when they had called him before them, he had bowed his obedience, and they had handed him the ultimate reward of the black belt. He had become a *shodan*, the lowest black-belt rank, but a member of the élite nonetheless.

Four days later an armed robber shot a filling-station attendant at night and in fleeing encountered a slender, unarmed Negro in street clothes. The robber had thrust out his arm to drive the harmless-looking man away and had received the greatest surprise he'd ever known just before sudden unconsciousness. He awoke much later in the prison ward of Los Angeles General Hospital with a broken arm in a plaster cast and the realization that he would shortly be back in Big Q for an extended stay.

That timely incident had marked the beginning of Tibbs' career as an investigator, which was the Pasadena Police Department's designation for certain of its detectives. On one of his first assignments he had worked as a shoeshine man for almost three weeks waiting for two men who were reported to meet there from time to time. When at last they had come, they had mistakenly assumed that the spiritless laborer working with the polish and brushes had no possible interest in their affairs. When he had finished their shines, he held out his hand, not for payment but to display a badge. At first they had not believed it; later they believed it completely, and for a short while, at least, one of the strands of the narcotics trade had been cut.

Tibbs, now the experienced professional, sat at his desk and went through a long file of missing-person reports. There were four possibles. He was noting them down when his phone rang and he was summoned to give a personal report to Captain Lindholm. He went gladly, but he had little to offer at that early stage beyond what was already on file.

"As I understand it, Virgil," the captain said, "the body was entirely nude, no clothing on it or nearby."

"No, sir," Tibbs replied.

"Anything useful at all in the way of ground marks?"

Tibbs shook his head. "The soil is very hard out there, sir. I made a careful check and found nothing."

"Then I assume there was not much to be found. Do you

see any connection between the nude body and the fact that it was found where it was?"

"No, sir, at least not at this point. The people who run the place appear responsible. They have a good reputation. The sheriff's office told me they have never had a complaint involving the nudist park—discounting crackpot calls, of course."

"Have you any ideas at this point?"

Tibbs hesitated. "Only in part. It seems pretty clear that the body was stripped and the dentures removed to give us a job making an identification."

"That seems logical, and except for the regular routine you haven't much to go on."

"There is one thing, sir." Tibbs put a small box on the captain's desk. "The murderer, if it was murder, overlooked something. I didn't call attention to it at the time because I didn't want to advertise the fact."

"What have you got, Virgil?"

Tibbs pointed to the little box. "Contact lenses," he said.

chapter 5

Whenever Virgil Tibbs spent a day, or a succession of days, of hard work without any fruitful result, he would refer to it as a "Yellow Face period." He drew his reference from Sherlock Holmes' famous adventure of *The Yellow Face* in which the immortal detective overreached himself, failed to come to the right conclusion, and ended up in humiliating defeat.

The next twenty-four hours constituted a Yellow Face period. Had the deceased been an itinerant-laborer type, he might never have been missed by anyone concerned enough to turn in a police report, but it was clear he had been a man of some substance and possibly even importance. Thus the normal expectation was that from some quarter an inquiry would come in concerning a missing person, who would turn out to be the body in the nudist-park pool. But no such person was reported missing.

Local fingerprint records were of no help, and the F.B.I. reported that it could not provide a make from its central files in Washington. Apparently the unknown man had never had his fingerprints taken, at least not in the United States.

Meanwhile Tibbs took another careful look at the four missing-person reports that he had already chosen as possibles.

A little work eliminated two of them; one was a decided long shot; the fourth offered some slight hope.

Then, at ten in the morning, a woman, who from her appearance could have been the dead man's wife, sailed with hesitant regality into the small lobby of the Pasadena police station and paused before the inquiry window.

"I would like to speak with a police officer," she announced with thin-lipped determination.

The desk man, who had been alerted, sensed a good possibility and summoned Tibbs. When the investigator arrived, the woman looked coolly at him and repeated herself almost exactly. "I would like to see a police officer."

"I am a police officer," Tibbs replied. "May I help you?"

The woman continued to regard him coolly. "I would like to speak to one of your *regular* officers."

"I am a regular officer, Ma'am."

"Perhaps, then, I should ask to see a detective."

At times, Tibbs' patience wore thin. Normally he controlled himself well, but the early frustrations of the day were already beginning to tell on him. "Madam," he said with enough firmness in his voice to convey authority, "*I* am a detective and am at your service. Now, what may I do for you?"

The woman stared at him for a moment, turned without a word, and walked out through the lobby doorway.

Tibbs bent over the drinking fountain to regain his self-control. He took hold of the sides of the fixture for a moment and the muscles of his fingers locked tight. When he straightened up, he was himself once more.

"Call me if anything else comes up, Harry," he said to the

man on duty. "If she comes back, try to find out what it's all about. If not, to hell with her."

Harry understood and nodded; things like this had happened before.

The morning mail brought a letter from Officer Sam Wood, of the Wells Police Department. With pardonable pride he informed Tibbs that his advancement to sergeant had been approved and would shortly take effect. Despite the fact that he had lived all his life in the South and was a Caucasian, Wood's was a very friendly letter. He reported that the music festival had been a definite success in Wells and that even the diehards now admitted that it had been a good idea. The town showed some few signs of reviving life due to the influx of tourist money. Miss Duena Mantoli, whom he had an engagement to see that evening, had specifically asked to be remembered, and sent her warm regards.

Tibbs slipped the letter into his pocket and felt infinitely better.

Missing person Number 4 on Tibbs' list was the possible. The subject had been a local resident and a personal call might be helpful. Tibbs called a number in the Eagle Rock area, reached the missing man's wife, and requested an appointment. Since it was only a short distance down the Colorado Freeway, he said he would be right over, fully aware that if the call resulted in anything positive, it would be his unfortunate duty to break the news to this woman that her husband was dead.

Mrs. Sean McCarthy, mother of five, confronted Tibbs through a hooked screen door and announced, "We're not in the market for anything."

"I'm the police officer who phoned you a few minutes ago, Mrs. McCarthy," Tibbs explained.

Very dubiously the woman unhooked the door and held it open to let him in. She was not tall—Tibbs guessed that she weighed about a hundred and sixty pounds. From the set of her jaw, he sensed that she could be a terror and that her temper probably lay just under the surface. Her eyes had a glittering hardness, though when she was young they might have been lovely. Her face was largely still smooth, but there were lines around her mouth already permanently sculptured into outlines of disapproval.

She made a cursory effort to be polite and motioned Tibbs to a vacant chair in the small living room. The furniture was pure borax, cheaply made with an effort to give it the appearance of massiveness. The upholstery was heavily studded with cloth-covered buttons intended to suggest elegance; when Tibbs sat down, the slight appearance of comfort dissolved.

Although he carefully tried to keep from jumping to unwarranted conclusions, he was already prepared for a disappointment. This home and this woman did not fit with the man whose body he had examined.

"The room isn't properly picked up yet," the woman said. "When you have five kids to look after and no man to help, you can't get everything done."

Tibbs felt a twinge of sympathy for her and approached the matter at hand as carefully as he could. "Mrs. McCarthy, something has come to our attention that might cast some light on your husband's disappearance." He decided to stretch the truth a little. "I take it from the appearance of your home that he is a man of some importance."

Mrs. McCarthy nodded firmly. "That he is," she agreed. "What have you discovered?"

Tibbs went on as delicately as possible, "We have a matter under investigation, and while there is very little chance it pertains to your husband, we don't want to overlook anything that might help to solve Mr. McCarthy's disappearance."

At last the woman showed a slight sign of approval. "Yes," she said.

Tibbs took the plunge. "Yesterday a distinguished-looking man was found, apparently the victim of an accident. He had no identification on his person, and so far we have not been able to establish who he was."

"He was dead, then?"

Tibbs nodded. "I fear so, Mrs. McCarthy, but I repeat, we have no real reason at all to believe that he was your husband."

The morning paper lay on the floor next to the chair Tibbs was sitting in. He picked it up, folded it to the story concerning the discovery of the body in the swimming pool, and silently handed it to his hostess. She took the paper and read the account without expression. When she was through, she laid it down as though it were something unclean. "That is not my husband," she announced, and the lines around her mouth set themselves firmly.

"May I ask how you know?" Tibbs inquired quietly.

Mrs. McCarthy took a deep breath, let it go, and clasped her arms in front of her generous bosom. "That body is not Mr. McCarthy," she reiterated, leaving no room whatever for question.

Tibbs framed his next words carefully and paced them

* 41

slowly, knowing that many people close their thoughts to lock out grief. "I'm sure that your opinion is correct, Mrs. McCarthy," he said, for the second time deliberately enlarging on the truth. "But for the sake of our official records it would be of great help if you would give me the reason for your conclusion."

If he had read her rightly, she was not the kind to be sparing of her advice. The desire to offer guidance might overcome her manifest unwillingness to discuss the body found in the pool. He watched while she struggled within herself, and knew the result before she spoke again.

"My husband," she said with unsinkable firmness, "would never be found, under any circumstances, in a place like *that*. We are respectable people here, Mr. Tibbett." She dropped her hands into her lap as though she were driving a pile.

Tibbs let a few seconds pass; then he made his voice flat and unemotional. "The people at the nudist resort made it very clear they didn't know the man who was found on their premises. He was neither a member nor a guest there."

"That is beside the point," Mrs. McCarthy said.

"What I am trying to say," Tibbs added, taking the blame upon himself, "is that the man obviously did not belong where he was found. Someone carried him there and put him into the pool."

The woman refused to yield. "I told you, and I see no need to repeat it, that we are an upright family and have nothing to do with places of public immorality. We are church people and we live our faith. My husband would never set foot in a nudist colony, dead or alive."

Tibbs knew better than to challenge a fixation head-on. He rose to his feet with the air that he was entirely convinced and satisfied. As he did so, the substantial housewife noted his apparent surrender and relaxed her guard.

Tibbs said, "While you are being so helpful, Mrs. McCarthy, there is one other thing that might assist us to resolve the matter of your husband's disappearance. Can you tell me if he had had his appendix removed?"

She shook her head. "No, he did not. He has never had surgery of any kind, unless it's been since he left home."

That nailed it down. "Thank you again for your cooperation, Mrs. McCarthy," Tibbs said in leaving. "From what you have told me, I am certain that the man we found is not your husband." This time, at least, he could speak the strict truth.

When he got back to his office, there was a preliminary phoned-in report from the San Bernardino medical examiner. It supplied the cause of death, a matter to which Tibbs gave his immediate full attention.

According to this first information, the unknown man had died as a result of a physical beating. All indications were that it had been a skilled assault; externally the body showed almost no signs of the abuse it had taken. A massive blow just below the breastbone, which had ruptured the aorta, was in all probability the major contributing cause of death. The deceased having been a good-sized man apparently in better-than-average physical condition, the person or persons who had caused his death had almost certainly been both powerful and well trained.

That put a fresh light on the matter. Any lingering thoughts of a morbid prank went out of Tibbs' mind. He swung his feet up onto the corner of the well-worn desk that had served many others before him, stared unseeing at the ceiling, and thought hard.

He was still in his position of deep concentration when his office mate came in. Tibbs was so fiercely involved in his thoughts that it was a good five minutes before he noticed his unofficial partner.

Bob Nakamura was ten pounds overweight and wore his thick black hair in a crew cut that emphasized the slight roundness of his face and figure. He did not have the buck teeth so commonly supposed to be a mark of Japanese ancestry, but he did wear glasses and with them a perpetual look of bland, innocent happiness. No one would have guessed he was a police detective, which added greatly to his value.

"How is it going?" Bob asked.

Tibbs pursed his lips before answering. "I think," he answered slowly, "I've just been able to figure out one thing that has been bothering me. Otherwise not so good. It's not as simple as I thought it was going to be."

Bob swung his chair around to face his colleague. "All right, unload. Give me all you've got and I'll see what I can make of it."

Tibbs got up, shut the door, and returned to his desk. "You know the basic facts. From these I put a few things together. First, the deceased had very distinct bathing-trunk marks, which substantiates the statement of the nudist-park people that he was not one of their members. This makes me think that the nudist angle is either purely accidental or else a deliberate red herring."

"I'd say the latter," Bob decided. "The coincidence of the nude body and the place where it was found is a little too strong."

"I'm inclined to agree, but don't forget that quite often dead bodies are found nude. Marilyn Monroe for example."

"Go on. I'm still listening."

"All right. Now, the swimming trunks he had been wearing were minimum briefs. Does that mean anything to you?"

"You tell me."

"Well, as you know, that kind of thing just isn't worn in this country, not even down on Muscle Beach. They are quite popular abroad, though, and are usually accepted over there. That makes me think that our man had been living overseas. The marks were so sharp and distinct I would infer a reasonably warm and sunny climate."

"Also that he was out a lot, on the beach or somewhere similar."

"Exactly, and since non-swimmers don't usually go in for that kind of brief, our man was probably well at home in the water. Either that or he was trying to show off, and he didn't look that type to me. No beard and none shaved off recently— no spectacular haircut, no tattoos, nothing of that sort at all."

"So he probably didn't drown."

"No, that's definite. He was expertly beaten to death. A blow in the solar plexus got him."

"Karate?" Bob suggested.

"Based on what I know of the art, I doubt it. The injuries apparently weren't that type. Just to be sure, when I get the detailed report, I'm going to see Nishiyama and ask him for an opinion."

"Good idea. Anything else to go on?"

"Mostly just guessing from here on out. He was well fed and apparently prosperous and successful. That combined with the deep suntan marks, which suggested a lot of leisure time, gave me the idea he might have been either a part-time high-salaried person like a movie director or else someone who had retired relatively young. That would add up if he were, say, an electronics engineer who had hit one or two good patents and was able to retire on the royalties."

"Problem," Bob interjected. "If he had been living abroad, then he could have been a Frenchman, a German, almost anyone."

"Unfortunately, you're right," Tibbs agreed. "The only solid fact I have to go on here is that his body was found in this country, which increases the chances that he was an American. Also his general appearance did not suggest a foreigner, except for the trunks. When we hit a trail, we can keep in mind that he may have had a foreign accent. But we can't tell that now."

"So you come back to the contact lenses."

"Right. I've been praying that someone would raise a howl about a missing person and we would have an answer the easy way. That could still happen, but I'm not banking on it."

Bob Nakamura folded his hands behind his head and took his turn at staring at the ceiling. "Obviously somebody has gone to a lot of trouble to hide this man's identity. The missing dental plates, and all that."

"No argument."

"The body was put into the pool at the nudist camp because it was—shall we say—appropriate. It would excite less comment being found there."

"No sale," Tibbs answered. "The club managers could prove fairly easily he wasn't theirs. Temporarily, at least, they have."

"They wanted the body to be found in a ridiculous place."

"No."

"The idea was to embarrass the camp—put it out of business."

"Possible, but doubtful. Too expert a murder job, for one thing."

"How's this: Suppose there were two people, which could well be: the actual murderer who dumped the body and someone else who found it. Say one man killed him and left the body on someone else's property. He didn't want to get involved, so he moved it to the nudist camp and left it there."

"Why not just drop it off a cliff in the first place?" Tibbs asked. "That whole area is loaded with wild canyons where disposal would be easy. After a few weeks, identification would have been even harder—a lot harder."

Bob tried a new tack. "You know, Virgil, there's something here that doesn't add up. On one hand, we agree there was a clear effort to make the body difficult to identify. On the other, it was left in a highly conspicuous place where it was sure to be found promptly."

Tibbs smiled with grim satisfaction. "That one stopped me cold on the scene," he admitted. "I tried to put it out of my mind, but it wouldn't go away. I've just been thinking about it."

"Any light?"

"Maybe." Tibbs got up and walked over to the window. "If an unidentified nude body is found on the premises of a nudist park, what is sure to result?"

"A police investigation."

"And what else?"

"A certain amount of publicity," Bob suggested.

Tibbs turned and faced him. "Exactly! In the Los Angeles

area a lot of people die violently—largely in traffic, but in other ways, too. A single isolated death of an unknown person isn't going to get much play in the papers unless the circumstances are unusual—in short, unless it adds up to a good story."

"And a body found floating in the pool at a nudist camp would definitely be unusual."

"I'd say spectacular," Tibbs added. "In most papers it would guarantee a good press coverage—perhaps even photos."

Bob thought that one over. "So the way you see it," he said after a good half minute, "there were two purposes here: to delay identification of the body as long as possible and, at the same time, to publicize the matter so that some person, or persons, would know what had happened."

Tibbs seated himself on the edge of Bob's desk. "It's the only way I can see it making sense. The man was killed for a purpose—obviously. Through the papers, someone somewhere is being told what happened, someone who knows who he was and why he died."

"When we find out who the dead man was, we may have a lead on finding that person. Until then, we're down to the contact lenses."

"Right." Tibbs locked his fingers together and stared at his hands—a characteristic gesture of his. "If it hadn't been for that oversight, we'd be waiting for something to come to us. Let's hope it pays off."

At two that afternoon Virgil Tibbs parked his inconspicuous black car in a space marked "VISITORS" adjacent to the plant of the Greenwood Optical Company. He showed his credentials to the receptionist and was ushered in promptly to see Arthur Greenwood, the sales manager, one of the three Greenwood brothers who owned and operated the company. That gentleman carefully examined the tiny lenses that Tibbs had brought with him, and became curious.

"How did you happen to come to us?" he asked.

"I know an optometrist in Pasadena," Tibbs explained. "He looked at the lenses and thought they might have been made by you."

Greenwood turned one of the small bits of plastic in his fingers. "Do you know anything about contact lenses?" he inquired.

"No," Tibbs answered. "I'll have to rely on you for help."

The executive leaned back in his swivel chair and prepared to lecture. "Today practically all lenses are taken from stock," he began. "Individual prescriptions seldom if ever need to be ground. In conventional eyeglasses every type of lens likely to be required is a stock item in all the shapes needed to fit various styles of frames. In contact lenses the field is much narrower. The number of different lenses available is much more restricted, and only a relatively limited range of prescriptions can be filled."

"In other words contact lenses aren't as distinctive as regular eyeglasses."

"Right. So your chance of tracing your man through these lenses is slim. However, you may have one advantage here: these are the vented type. There are a number of contact-lens makers, but the vented ones are relatively uncommon. We are one of the better sources in this country."

"Are there many abroad?"

"Oh, yes, some of course—mainly in Europe and in Japan, where contact lenses were invented. From these I can't tell you for certain whether we made them or not."

"Assuming that you did," Tibbs pursued patiently, "would you have any way of determining for whom they were made? Or would they be simply a stock item, as you said?"

Greenwood pondered the question. "We might—and I stress *might*—be able to tell you who prescribed them, but our records normally are confidential."

"I can obtain a court order if you need one," Virgil answered. "However, since this is a murder investigation and time is an important element, I would like to ask for your cooperation."

His ego and conscience satisfied, Greenwood buzzed for his secretary. "Have these lenses checked in the shop," he directed. "Find out if you can who we made them for. If you can't do that, find out about how many similar sets we have made in this style."

The girl took the box with the lenses and closed the door behind her. Greenwood made small talk until she returned a few minutes later. She put the box on his desk and with it a slip of paper.

Greenwood read it and nodded. "We are very fortunate," he said. "The lenses are quite distinctive; one eye is very different from the other and that isn't too common. Now, understand that I can't guarantee we made these lenses. However . . ." He picked up the paper and studied it again for a second or two, clearly for dramatic effect. "We did manufacture a set of lenses to this exact prescription within the last two years. I don't have the patient's name, of course, but the order came from Dr. Nathan Shapiro. He's very well known here in the contact-lens field."

Virgil Tibbs had an almost uncontrollable desire to stand

up and shout. Instead he rose, expressed his thanks, praised the company's efficiency, and escaped to his car. He stopped at the first phone booth, consulted the yellow pages, and was on his way.

Dr. Shapiro's white-frocked receptionist regarded him as a curiosity. "Doctor is very busy this afternoon," she informed him. "I doubt very much he will be able to see you." There were patients waiting who bore out her statement.

Tibbs reached into his wallet and produced a card, a considerably less conspicuous procedure than showing his badge. The girl looked at it, then back at him, and laid the card down. "You'll have to wait," she said.

Tibbs sat down and waited. He leafed through the outdated magazines, read a pamphlet on eye care, and noted the studied coolness of the receptionist, who was making an effort to pretend he was not there. Some time after the last of the waiting patients had been shown in, she picked up the phone and pressed the intercom button. When the answer came, she spoke in a tone so low Tibbs could not catch a sound. He did not need to; he knew without watching the words her lips were forming.

Ten minutes later Dr. Shapiro came into the waiting room. He was a big man with a round face and a sharply receding hairline that gave him the look of having been polished. He wore the customary white jacket, which set off a pair of big muscular hands the backs of which were almost covered with black hair. He walked directly to Tibbs with a brusqueness that allowed no time for casual talk.

"I'm sorry I haven't been able to take time to see you," he said directly. "I suggest you phone for an appointment. It may be some time. I seldom see anyone in less than thirty days."

"I'm not a patient," Tibbs answered. "I came on official police business."

The doctor glanced at his receptionist; when he looked back, Tibbs was holding out his shield. "I didn't understand," the doctor said. "Come in. I'll take a few minutes now."

Once he grasped the situation, Dr. Shapiro listened carefully, looked at the lenses, and instructed his receptionist to check the records. She checked and supplied the name of Mr. Michael Casella, president of the Casella Construction Company. Mr. Casella had once sustained a minor eye injury that had required a later radical correction of his vision.

Although it was late in the day, Tibbs borrowed the office phone long enough to call the Casella Construction Company. Mr. Casella was not in; he had not been in for the past several days. His secretary was not certain where he was; she believed he was out in the field inspecting construction sites.

Struggling to keep his voice normal, Virgil made an appointment for nine the following morning. Then he went home to enjoy the fruits of his labors.

Precisely on time the next morning, he drove into the yard of the Casella Construction Company and parked his car on the unpaved area before the white clapboard building that was the office. There were several large pieces of earth-moving equipment standing in the yard and a small assortment of cars. Among them was a Lincoln Continental; when he saw it, Tibbs frowned.

Inside the door there was a railing that separated the working area from the few square feet set aside for a lobby. Tibbs presented himself to the receptionist-typist-switchboard operator and asked if Mr. Casella was in.

Without replying the girl plugged in a cord and said, "Someone to see Mike."

A middle-aged and ample woman, who looked as if she might be a bookkeeper, appeared and asked, "Are you the man who phoned last night?"

After Tibbs replied, she opened the railing gate for him and showed him into the single corner office. From behind the desk, a powerful man with a thick tangle of black hair on his head offered a fast handshake and motioned toward a wooden chair. "I didn't get your name," he said.

"Tibbs. Virgil Tibbs."

"Mike Casella, Virgil. What's your line?"

Tibbs produced his card.

"Cop, heh? O.K., what's the beef?"

"No beef, just two fast questions. One—do you wear contact lenses?"

"Yep, love 'em to death. If you want some, I can give you the name of a damn good doctor—Nat Shapiro. Really knows his stuff."

"Thanks. One more—have you lost or misplaced a set of lenses recently?"

Casella pulled two cigars from his pocket and offered one to Tibbs, who declined. "Nope. I only have one set and I've got them on now. I know you can't see 'em—nobody can. Great invention. What's it all about?"

He was entitled to an answer. "We found a man dead with lenses similar to yours. We wanted to be sure you were O.K., that's all."

"Well, fine," Casella answered. "About those kids that were hanging around the yard. If you catch 'em, give 'em a good scare and then let them go. They can't hurt the equipment, but they can hurt themselves and then we're in trouble." He stopped. "And thanks for the protection. Stop around before Christmas. We like to keep in touch with our friends."

Tibbs shook hands and left. Halfway across the yard he saw a golf-ball-sized stone in his path, drew back his right foot, and kicked at it with vicious power. He missed a square-on kick; the stone skidded a few feet to the side and stopped.

He got into his car and sat motionless for a moment, his frustration settling in him like a huge leaden lump. "Damn," he said between his teeth. He was in no fit mood for anything as he drove toward the civic center and his waiting office.

chapter 6

For the next twenty-four hours Virgil Tibbs lived in a world of hope. He kept a close and continuous vigil over all sources of information concerning missing persons and reviewed crime reports in the hope of finding some faint connection with the body in the pool. He checked with other law-enforcement agencies throughout California, Nevada, and Arizona. At the end of another day of concentrated effort he drew a complete and absolute blank.

Meanwhile in the morgue in San Bernardino the body of an unknown man rested on a slab, unclaimed and yielding no clue that might lead to an identification. The most frustrating thing about the whole stalemate was that no one seemed to care. No anxious wife phoned in anywhere to ask about a missing husband; no business associates made inquiry. The man, whoever he had been, seemed to have lived in a vacuum.

People, Tibbs decided, seldom gave a damn about one another. Landlords weren't concerned about their tenants so long as the rent was paid. Neighbors were not much inclined to be neighborly any more. Most car drivers had little sympathy for others on the road. And often when a serious crime had been committed, few citizens would come forward to help the police; they were too afraid of getting involved.

Tibbs thrust the image of such cases out of his mind. When things went against him, his brain seemed to delight in torturing him by exhuming every awkward and wretched incident he had ever known in his lifetime. They paraded in front of him, the zombies of things long since dead come back to haunt him. The mistakes be had made, the breaks that had gone against him, and the countless times he had been forced to accept humiliation he did not deserve simply because he was a Negro.

Inaction was killing him; he had to do something. The longer he sat in his office, the more likely it was that Captain Lindholm would drop in to ask how soon he would have the case closed. Finally, with no clear idea of what good would come of it, he got out his car, stopped for gas, and then turned eastward on Highway 66. He cleared the outskirts of Pasadena, passed the Santa Anita race track, and worked his way through Azusa. Then he picked up speed and rolled along the foothills of the mountains. The sun, which had been obscured by a low overcast, broke through when he passed Claremont and his spirits responded to the opening cheerfulness of the sky.

He turned off at the secondary road, drove another ten miles on the hardtop, and turned in at the entrance of Sun Valley Lodge. The chain was not up and he was able to negotiate the S turn through the shrubbery directly to the parking lot. Today several other cars were there; when he shut the engine off, he could hear the unmistakable sounds of children at play coming from the direction of the pool area.

He got out of the car wondering a little why he had come. On the surface he knew the answer; he *had* to find a new lead. But he admitted to himself that he had no idea where to look. He was convinced that the Nunns were on the level and were not holding out on him. A severe cross-examination, particularly on their premises, was not in order. He would therefore begin by asking if anything new had happened or been discovered. After they had said no to that, he would retrace everything again, looking for something he might have missed the first time.

He was only a few feet down the path that led to the house when Forrest arrived to greet him. Tibbs sensed instantly that his welcome was genuine.

"Hello, Virgil," the park director said. "Pardon my using your first name, but that is the universal custom in nudist parks."

"That's fine," Tibbs said. He noted that his host was again wearing bleached-out khaki shorts, apparently his standard costume for meeting visitors at the parking lot.

Forrest led the way into the big kitchen, where Emily was preparing an immense bowl of tomato-studded tossed salad. "Why, Virgil," she greeted him. "How nice you're back. You'll have lunch with us, won't you?"

"Yes, he will," Forrest supplied before Tibbs could speak. He drew two cups of coffee and set them on the table.

Tibbs wanted to explain that this was an official call, not a social one. He opened his mouth to do so and then had sense enough to close it again. These people knew that, but they were treating him as a guest anyway. He was a person just like them, welcome to go anywhere and do anything that anyone else might do. It was like walking through the gates into Paradise.

He looked down at his ebony hands and hated them.

Carole came into the room, so well browned all over her

smooth little body that apart from her blue eyes she might have been a distand relative of his. She greeted him with childish enthusiasm, and Tibbs, when he looked at her with his own dark-brown eyes, felt his heart stir.

Forrest helped him over a hurdle. "I know you want to talk to us, Virgil, and of course we're available. If you could wait a few minutes until after lunch, it would help. We have guests on the grounds today."

Tibbs agreed, realizing that he had unintentionally foisted himself on them for lunch. He should have said something about having already eaten, but at eleven-thirty in the morning it would have been unrealistic and they might have been offended. It was then he considered the fact that these people, being nudists, must have known the sting of prejudice, too. With them it was voluntary, but there must have been times when they had had to bear public ridicule and scorn. That would be the face it would wear, but their real transgression was the same one he was guilty of—being different. In a civilization where people who are different are sometimes richly rewarded, and even have temples built for them on the banks of the Potomac, he knew they are more often hated and despised for their lack of sameness.

Why, Tibbs wondered, is being exactly like everyone else so often taken for a great virtue? The world depended on people being different; otherwise it couldn't run. There had to be leaders and there had to be workers. There had to be businessmen, artists, engineers, cops, architects, and people willing to work in slaughterhouses and rendering plants. There had to be farmers and possibly also politicians. People to do the imposing, exalted work and people to do the dirty, unpleasant work; and they couldn't be the same people.

His thinking was interrupted when George came in. For a moment Tibbs felt the young man should have been wearing shorts in the presence of his mother. Virgil rose and greeted George a little awkwardly; his recent mental wandering had him off balance. "For gosh sakes, take off your coat, Virgil," George urged. "It's warm today and you don't need all those clothes on."

Then Tibbs realized that he felt strange not only because of his color, but also because he was fully dressed in a business suit in this place where attire was functional and no more. "I'd be glad to get rid of the coat," he admitted. He removed it carefully and hung it across the back of his chair.

"We've got thirty-four now," George informed his apron-clad mother. "Abe and Sarah came in and so did Don and Pam."

Emily nodded and took it in her stride. "We prepare the food here," Forrest explained, "and then take it over to the dining hall on weekdays, when it doesn't pay to open up the big kitchen."

Tibbs watched as Emily swung open the oven and removed several large dishes, rich with satisfying aroma. George carried them to the doorway and set them on a kind of serving table on wheels that was pulled up outside. When all but one had been loaded, he took off with the cart across the grass. At this point, when many housewives would have stopped to wipe their foreheads, Emily simply smiled and said to her unexpected guest, "We'll eat right away. George and Linda will take care of the guests and then be right up. We keep all the bread and things like that stored in the dining-hall food lockers. It works out very well that way."

Tibbs felt that a confession was in order. "When I came,

I didn't realize the hour—my mind was on other things. Let me come back later this afternoon when you won't be so rushed."

"Nonsense," Emily retorted quickly. "We can all sit around the table and talk. 'Good food begets good ideas,' my father used to say."

Still feeling out of place, but grateful for his reception, Tibbs watched the smooth efficiency with which Emily set the places for lunch and put out the things that would be needed on the table. She seemed to do everything easily; she wasted no motion. She was almost finished when Tibbs glanced out the window and his thoughts stopped dead in their tracks.

George and Linda were coming. Obviously she knew that he was there; George would have told her. Nonetheless she walked easily beside her brother, to all appearances entirely unconcerned and totally nude except for a pair of sandals on her feet.

She was coming toward the kitchen and in a few seconds would be in the room.

Tibbs was engulfed with a reminder of his heritage. The vast canyon that onetime servitude had eroded between his people and the Caucasian race had been so impressed on him during his boyhood in the Deep South that the sight of a naked white woman was a severe shock. For a Negro even speaking to a white woman under some circumstances could be suspect in Mississippi; the Till murder had come from a simple thing like that.

Linda was eighteen years old and, as Tibbs had previously noted, well formed. He had even considered her as a possible motive for murder; such things had happened before. She was rich with the promise of womanhood and technically over the age of consent.

"Here they come now," Forrest said.

Tibbs grasped at the thought that she would go in by another door and slip on a dress before appearing for lunch. But instantly he knew it was not so; she would come in just the way she was.

George held the door open for his sister. She entered the room with such easy grace that Tibbs, for a reason he could not explain, was instantly reminded of Beethoven's Sixth Symphony.

It was noon on a bright and beautiful day and the girl who had entered the room was beautiful. It was not the artificiality of a carefully made-up face and an elaborate hair style emerging above the creation of an important couturier; it was the natural beauty of young womanhood of the kind that had stirred Praxiteles and countless other artists in the twenty-four centuries that had followed.

As Tibbs automatically rose to his feet, she came to greet him. "Welcome back, Mr. Tibbs. Do you mind if I call you Virgil?"

He dared to smile at her. "If you like. It's a little hard to be formal—under the circumstances—isn't it?"

She smiled back and was radiant. "Good. Have you come to tell us that you've caught the murderer?"

Tibbs shook his head. "I've come to tell you that I need some more of your help."

He meant the "your" to be plural; she took it as singular.

"Wonderful. I'd love it. Right after lunch, whatever you want."

As she turned and went to help her mother, Tibbs could

not help watching her. The symmetry of her body was perfect and the curve at the small of her back made him wish fervently that he was a painter.

Emily Nunn served lunch and they sat down to eat. As he took his seat, Tibbs felt himself badly out of place. He picked up his napkin and put it in his lap with self-conscious motions. He had not often been invited for a meal in a white home, seldom if ever while on an official errand, and positively never under the circumstances that surrounded him now. Also his usual lunch was a sandwich and a milk shake, which made him uncertain that he could do justice to the heartier fare that was being set before him now.

To his surprise he found that he was hungry and the home-cooked food, of a sort he seldom got, whetted his appetite. Linda, who sat opposite him, kept up a more or less running conversation on the general subject of police work. Whether it was intentional or not, it put him a little more at ease to talk about the subject he knew best; he answered her questions frankly and everyone present seemed to be interested.

Eventually he decided to take the Nunns partly into his confidence. "I have a serious problem in this case," he explained. "I don't want it to go beyond this room, but as of now I can't identify the body."

"You mean that no one has reported the man missing?" Emily asked.

"Exactly. No inquiry at all has come in from anywhere in this tri-state area, nor anything else that might be helpful. I can tell you now that when he was found he was wearing a set of almost invisible contact lenses. When I traced them down, they led nowhere and I'm right back where I started."

"Glasses! So that's what you held out on me," Linda said.

"One of the things, yes."

"Was an autopsy performed?" Forrest asked.

"Yes, but it gave us very little we didn't already have. Nothing significant. I don't want to discuss it at the table, but in general terms the findings were routine." That was all he cared to tell them; he wasn't going to go into the cause of death.

Emily reached for a serving dish and without asking his permission added more baked salmon to his plate. Tibbs politely protested and then was grateful, for it was delicious.

"How can we help you?" Forrest asked.

Tibbs cut off a portion of the fish with his fork and looked up. "Actually I'm not sure that you can," he said. "I could make a big show of asking a lot of questions, but the truth is I came back to see if I could get another lead—something that was overlooked the first time." He stopped and ate a mouthful of food. Then he went on, "I can tell you this: it won't be anything glaring. It will be some minor thing, something that seemed so unimportant it didn't even come up."

"I want to ask something," George put in. "Suppose there just isn't any such lead and the man remains unidentified. What then?"

Tibbs drank a wonderfully cooling half glass of iced tea without coming up for air. It was such magic in his throat that he did not want to stop. "Because it's murder," he said finally, "the case will technically remain open. All murder cases do until they are solved. But if nothing turns up, then I'll have to go on to something else. There are always new problems in police work. Perhaps in a few weeks something might break, or even at the end of a year."

"But if not?" George persisted.

"Then the murderer gets away with it and goes scot free. It happens all the time. I don't like to say that, but it's true."

"I want the man who killed the man in our pool to be caught," Linda said. "I can't stand the idea that he could do what he did and not have to pay for it."

"If we're going to catch him," Tibbs said, "I'll need all the help you can give me."

"Then it's up to us to go over every detail in our minds and look for every bit of information, no matter how remote," Forrest said. "Even if we can't be sure it's right."

Virgil finished the iced tea and enjoyed the cool touch of the ice cubes against his lips. Linda got up and refilled his glass. He leaned back as she did so, freshly aware of her nudity.

"It won't be easy," he said when Linda had finished and returned to her chair. "But we have to try."

"Where shall we begin?" Emily asked.

Self-conscious again, Tibbs carefully stirred a spoonful of sugar into his tea and added a slice of lemon. "Let's begin with the area you know best," he proposed. "I've been going on the assumption that there is no nudist angle in this case, that the body was found in your pool more or less by coincidence."

He stopped, momentarily at a loss for words. "I accepted that idea because if I could help it I didn't want to damage your business and its good will. I realize that it must be hard to build up a clientele for this type of operation—to win community acceptance."

Forrest crossed his long legs under the table and relaxed back in his chair. "In a way, yes," he acknowledged. "But it's not as hard as you might think. We get a lot of inquiries. People are beginning to realize, for example, that kids with a nudist background have a wholesome, healthy attitude toward their bodies. They don't play the wrong kind of games in a corner of the garage."

He looked up at his wife and smiled. "I could tell you a lot more. For instance, nudist families have a much lower divorce rate than the rest of the population. But that's not what you are interested in now. If there *is* a nudist angle to this case, you can count on us for all possible help to try and find it. Having the thing settled and done would be infinitely better than to have the matter permanently hanging over our heads."

From the tone of his voice, Tibbs believed him. It seemed reasonably certain that none of the family would try to hold out information, unless, of course, it was coupled with guilty knowledge. That was a possibility he was not yet ready to dismiss.

"All right, then," he said. "Let's start with the premise that the deceased wasn't a practicing nudist because of the very marked pattern of his bathing trunks." He looked toward Linda and relaxed his seriousness for a moment. "Because he was a cottontail."

Linda nodded her approval. She was resting her chin on her hands, with her elbows on the table. In that position her breasts were partially covered and Tibbs noted, to his embarrassment, that the unconscious partial concealment automatically invited more attention to that part of her body.

He got back rapidly to the logic of the case. "Isn't it true that everyone who is a nudist had to start sometime?" he asked. "Certainly not everyone who comes here now began as a little child."

"That's right," Emily agreed. "Only a small percentage of today's nudists grew up in the movement."

"Then isn't it possible that our unknown man was about to become a nudist—or had been one for, say, a day or two?"

Linda drew a breath quickly. "I can answer the second part. He hadn't been a nudist at all—at least not this summer—or it would show. Of course, he could have been at a park some-where on a dark and gloomy day, but it's very unlikely. And even one day in the sun would have tanned him a little. He was too white for that."

"How about an overcast day, but one that was still pleas-ant?" Tibbs asked. "There are lots of those." He looked at his dark fingers. "I'm at a slight disadvantage here," he admit-ted.

Forrest understood at once and took over. "A person with a very fair skin, such as he had, can be severely sunburned even on a cloudy day. Every experienced nudist knows this. It happens to newcomers all the time, even though we warn them."

"Dad's right," George added, nodding his head.

Tibbs went on, "Then he wasn't a nudist, at least not re-cently. But is there any reason why he might not have been planning to become one? He liked the out-of-doors or he wouldn't have had so deep a suntan."

"That's a definite possibility," George said. "Unfortunately, so far only a small percentage of people have decided to be-come nudists, but the number is steadily going up. He was a better class individual, I think, and that increases the possibil-ity since that's the kind we usually attract."

Tibbs looked questioningly at Forrest, who nodded his

head. "That's a proven fact," he added. "Though some people might doubt it."

"Then he could have been on his way here when he was killed. It's even possible that he had arrived and was ambushed before he could announce himself."

"I don't think so," Carole answered.

Emily turned toward her younger daughter, smiled, and then placed a finger across her lips to indicate that she should remain quiet.

Tibbs looked down at the little girl, on his left. "Why not, Carole?" he asked.

"Because he didn't have a reservation. If he was a smart man, wherever he was going he would have a reservation." She ended on a note of righteous indignation; she did not like to be shushed when she had an idea.

Tibbs pressed his palm against his forehead. "I'm ashamed of myself," he said. "I never thought of that. Because of his suntan marks and the lack of any fingerprint record in this country, I was pretty sure he had come from abroad, but I couldn't check the airline records because I didn't have anything to go on. The reservation angle I completely missed."

" Did I help?" Carole asked.

"Indeed you did. You are wonderful—what can I do for you?"

Because she had been thinking much about the dark detective since he had first appeared, Carole was ready immediately with her answer. "I want to ride in a police car," she announced. "With the siren going."

Tibbs smiled and got quickly to his feet. "I've got to go," he said. "Thank heaven there's work to be done. Thank you for my lunch—I seldom have one so good. Thanks also for the cooperation. You especially, Carole, and I won't forget what you asked."

"I'm jealous," Linda said, smiling to show that she didn't mean it.

Tibbs looked at her, somewhat more accustomed now to her lack of clothing. "You'll never need to be jealous of anyone," he declared without emphasis. He put his coat over his arm and left.

Linda watched him as he retreated across the lawn toward his car, "You know," she said, "he's quite a man."

"I like him," Forrest answered. "He's a gentleman and a very intelligent one."

"The girl who gets him will be pretty lucky," Linda mused.

Her mother gave her a quick, surprised glance that had in it a touch of concern. Although Linda was not looking at her, the girl read the reaction and understood it. "I assume he would prefer a Negro girl, but they want good men, too, don't they?"

Emily Nunn relaxed the touch of tension that had appeared on her face. "I'm certain of it," she agreed.

chapter 7

When Virgil Tibbs walked into his office at close to three in the afternoon, Bob Nakamura took one look at the face of his Negro associate and knew that he had got his teeth into something. "Identify the body?" he asked.

"No," Virgil answered shortly. "But I have got an angle to try, and it might work. Are you busy?"

Bob leaned back, clasped his hands behind his head, and beamed. "Shoot," he invited.

"I want to trace down all the likely places where a man arriving from overseas within the past week or ten days might have had a reservation and didn't pick it up. Or where he did check in and then disappeared. The first is the best bet, because if he had walked out and left his luggage or his bill behind him, we'd hear of it."

"Nice idea," Bob agreed. "But it's worse than doing the pawnshops—just too many places around here that take reservations. How many hotels and motels do you think there are in Los Angeles alone?"

"I know," Tibbs answered, "but there is an end to it somewhere, particularly when you cut out the second- and third-class spots."

"Are you going to do just L.A. or all the rest of the basin?"

Tibbs dropped into his chair, letting his weight fall. "I'm

going to go the whole route and ask for the cooperation of all of the law-enforcement agencies between here and Palmdale. Ask them to check every likely spot where a well-to-do man might make a reservation. I'll start myself with the big places, like the Beverly Hilton, that a stranger might pick out of a travel guide or an agency might line up. But I don't know that he was a stranger; he might have had a favorite spot he always used. If I read him right, that's a good chance, too."

"Needle in a haystack," Bob commented agreeably.

"I know it, but at least there's only one haystack. Want to help?"

The benign look left Bob's face. "Let's get going," he said.

Despite the warmth of early summer, the air in the San Bernardino Mountains had a touch of crispness and the subtle scent of many growing plants that had found a home above five thousand feet. Here on the rolling plateau behind the first range of the mountains time moved with less urgency. The roads were more casual and wound their way with dignity, satisfied to handle light traffic at thirty miles an hour. The frantic drive of the ramrod freeways did not exist here; the buildings scattered among the trees were principally cottages with occasional small establishments suited to the more leisurely life of a semirural vacation area. Yet in spite of the outward appearance of a calmer world, the whole area was laced with modern communications, power-distribution lines, and occasional special facilities for defense and air-traffic control.

A pleasant thing about driving on one of the roads through this lightly wooded, lightly settled area was the fact that the birds could be heard singing. The rush of the wind was absent, and the sounds of nature could penetrate even into the hostile atmosphere of an automobile. Officer Richard Mooney noted all this and enjoyed it. He was an impressive figure in his California Highway Patrol uniform, which radiated authority. The official car he was driving ran beautifully and seemed, like him, to be responding to the perfect day. Though his uniform was a little warm and his feet in particular were uncomfortable from the tight embrace of too much leather, he was relaxed and contented.

He was on a routine checkup that involved no problems. He was in love with his job, and although the pay was less than it should have been, he was human enough to enjoy the aura of authority and the sense of being a member of an élite group that the job gave him. He was a friendly man, but he maintained a careful distance between himself and others so that his position as part of the long arm of the law would not be compromised.

He had so far stopped at eight resorts without success. He was not disappointed, as he had expected nothing. In police work, he knew, much time and effort had to be futilely spent. It was part of his responsibility to do his share.

He pulled into the gravel driveway of one of the more elaborate spots, shut the car door firmly, and went inside. He was back out again shortly—negative. He noted the name of the place on his report sheet, slipped the car into gear, and moved smoothly on.

A half mile more brought him to the next place, which was small but neat and attractive. The drive was packed earth this time, with a scattering of pine needles from the tree branches overhead; the pattern of light and shade across the entrance was exactly right for the kind of place it was. Dick Mooney, who did not live in the immediate area, decided that this would be a nice spot for a short vacation sometime. It would be certain to please his wife, Elaine. From the outside, at least, it was just the sort of place she liked. He pulled his car to a stop, got out, and walked to the door.

A slender girl met him behind the desk. She matched the place perfectly, subdued but appealing. She wore a simple dress and very little makeup. Her light-chestnut hair had a natural look that suggested that all she had to do was brush and comb it in the morning and it would look fine all day.

Dick Mooney took off his uniform cap and let his face show that this was an official, but not necessarily unpleasant, errand. "Good morning, Miss," he said with some formality. "I'm making a routine check through the area."

"Are we in any trouble?" the girl asked.

"Not that I know of," he reassured her. "I only want to ask you a question about reservations. I presume you take them here?"

"Yes, we do," she answered. "Most of our guests—at least during the season—come by reservation. Some make them a full year ahead."

Mooney put his cap down on the counter for a moment and consulted the clipboard in his hand. "Within the last two weeks has any guest who had a reservation failed to appear? In particular, a man of about fifty or so who may have been coming in from overseas, but not necessarily so."

The girl shook her head. "No," she answered. "Everyone who had reservations is here with the exception of the Hacketts; they phoned and canceled. They are quite young—in their late twenties or early thirties, at the most."

Dick wrote down the name of the resort on his report sheet. "Thank you," he said. "They wouldn't be the people."

Because his manner was pleasant and because she wanted to be sure of his continued good will, the girl saw him to the door. "We have a very quiet place here," she explained. "Most of our guests come back to us year after year. They aren't usually the kind who get into trouble."

The anxiety in her voice caused him to say, "It isn't that. We're looking for someone who is missing, that's all." It wasn't the exact truth, he knew, but it was easier said that way.

The girl let her shoulders drop a trifle to indicate that she was no longer concerned. "Well, everyone we expected is here apart from the Hacketts, as I told you, and none of our guests would fit your description except Uncle Albert, and we're never sure when we'll see him."

"Thank you for your trouble," he concluded, and got back into his car. It was the last stop and he turned back toward the station.

He reported in briefly. "All negative."

It was the expected answer and the duty man nodded. Mooney took the sheet off his clipboard and turned it in; that finished the job and he was free of it.

"Nothing at all in the whole area," the duty man told him. That was expected, too, but usually the men working on something like to know the outcome. It would have stopped there forever if he had not added "Not even a nibble" for the sake of something to say.

That touched a slight recent memory in Mooney's mind. "A girl at Pine Shadows Lodge said something about expecting an uncle who fitted the description, but she didn't know when to look for him." His conscience was clearer for having put in this bit of added information.

Later in the day, the duty man reported back to Pasadena. "A full check of the area was negative," he advised. He debated the idea of saying any more; it would probably do nothing but give somebody extra trouble. But because he was proud of the efficiency of his unit and basically liked to talk, he added, "We have one place that *might* be expecting someone who fits your description, but there's no ETA on him."

"O.K. Thank you."

The full report, including the fragmentary comment, was passed on to Bob Nakamura, who was correlating the incoming information for Tibbs. When Virgil at last came in, footweary, at six, Bob was there to give him the report. "Practically everything is in," he said. "All negative. One small place up in the mountains is expecting someone who fits the description, but no definite time of arrival."

"From overseas?" Tibbs asked.

"I gathered so. There weren't any details."

"What was the name of the place?"

In the fresh coolness of the next morning the girl sat quietly at her small desk beside a half-open screened window and carefully filled in the figures on the week's expense record. The light wind stirred the pine branches overhead just enough to give a sense of something moving in an otherwise static world. With business-like care she sorted the bills she had before her; after each bill had been entered, she turned it upside down to keep them in sequence. When a chime sounded indicating that someone had crossed the electric doormat at the front entrance, she finished the entry she was making and rose to meet her visitor.

As she stepped through the doorway into the small lobby,

she saw that the caller was a well-dressed, rather slim Negro. Her first thought was that he was looking for work. Whatever his errand, she took her place behind the counter and said "Good morning" with exactly the right degree of restraint.

"Good morning," the Negro answered, and those two words revealed that he had been educated. "I didn't see your sign. Is this Pine Shadows Lodge?"

He was not, therefore, casually looking for work. "Yes, it is," she replied. "I'm sorry about the sign. Apparently a car knocked it down last night. It was on a post by the gate and we haven't had time to put it back up."

The Negro took out his wallet, extracted a small white card, and laid it on the desk before her. She looked down at it, and her mind moved forward rapidly. He was from the Pasadena Police Department, but Pasadena was many miles away. In any problem involving the lodge, the sheriff would be in charge. The only reasonable assumption, then, was a solicitation for some police-sponsored benefit. If so, the Pasadena people were ranging very far indeed from their normal area. It occurred to her that they had deliberately sent a Negro to make turning him down slightly more embarrassing. The accounts that she had been working on told her the state of the lodge's finances; she would give him a dollar and conclude the matter.

"What can I do for you, Mr. Tibbs?" she asked politely.

"I would like to ask you a few questions, if I may," he answered. "Would you give me your name?"

At that the girl tensed a bit. Her prognosis had clearly been wrong and she did not know what to expect. She was the kind of person who liked to do things calmly and in proper order.

"I am Ellen Boardman." It was all he had asked, and it was all she answered.

He glanced at her left hand, which was devoid of jewelry. "Are you an employee of the lodge, Miss Boardman?" His voice was courteous, but she did not like the question; it was an invasion of her private life, which she preferred to keep to herself.

"You might say that. My parents own it. I'm managing it for them in their absence."

He sensed her restraint, the coolness in her voice. "Miss Boardman, the matter I am currently investigating is quite serious. There is only a remote chance that it might involve this lodge or you, but that possibility does exist."

Her first reaction was almost automatic: if the matter was so serious, why had they sent this Negro man? Then the full impact of his words reached her and she was a little frightened.

"What has happened?" she asked. "Are my parents all right?" Her voice climbed out of its accustomed smoothness and became audibly tight and tense. "Has there been an accident?"

"I don't believe your parents are involved," he said quickly. He stopped there and gave her a moment to recover herself. She looked down and saw that her hands were clenched; consciously she relaxed them and rested them on the counter. She looked up as a signal that he was to go on.

"Yesterday, I believe, an officer stopped in to see you concerning any reservations you might have had that weren't either canceled or picked up. You mentioned something to him about expecting someone else—a relative or a member of the family."

It tied in now, and she blamed herself for talking too much. She raised her hand and brushed her hair back from her cheek. "I'm terribly sorry," she answered. "I hope you didn't come all the way up here just on account of that."

"Please tell me who you were expecting," Tibbs said.

Her sense of restraint rushed back upon her, but now she had no choice. "I was referring to my Uncle Albert," she replied, still annoyed with herself. "My mother's brother. He's retired and prefers to spend most of his time overseas. He comes to visit us every summer."

"How old a man is he?" Tibbs asked.

"Fifty-two."

"Can you describe him?"

A certain sense of foreboding that had been lurking in the back of her mind began to take hold of her. She thought before she spoke. "I guess he's about five feet eleven—just under six feet, I'd say. He's fully built—not fat, but substantial. Perhaps he weighs a hundred and eighty or a hundred and ninety pounds, but that's just a guess. I haven't seen him for a year, you understand."

Tibbs nodded. "Can you tell me anything about his eyesight?"

"His— Well, he wears glasses," she said. "He has for years. Actually he has trouble with only one eye. It was injured in a laboratory many years ago." She thought for a moment. "Well—he may not be wearing glasses now," she added. "He wrote us a few months ago that he was trying out contact lenses, and apparently he liked them very much."

"When were you expecting him?" Tibbs asked quietly.

"I don't really know. About this time—no definite date. He just wrote he was going to visit some people in England and then come here in time for the board meeting."

"Do you know the date of the meeting?"

She looked at a small desk calendar on the counter. "Three weeks from today," she answered slowly. Her words formed involuntarily; she had just realized the man had asked about her uncle's eyesight, and that was a very specific question. She forced herself to ask the thing she dreaded; it could have a terrible answer.

"Has something happened to him?"

"Do you by any chance have a picture of him available?" Tibbs asked in return.

She was aware that he had side-stepped the question. "Only some snapshots taken here a year ago." She looked anxiously at him.

Tibbs nodded. The girl turned quickly and retreated into her living quarters. She did not have to search; in her room things were in place. She was back within a minute with some small glossy prints in her hand. Her fingers shook as she handed them over.

Tibbs glanced at the top one. "Suppose we sit down," he proposed.

Mechanically the girl came from behind the counter and settled into one of the few chairs in the lobby.

When she was seated, Tibbs chose a position a short distance from hers. Then, his face revealing nothing, he carefully looked at each of the snapshots. They were clear and good. When he had finished, he laid the pictures down, and somehow at that moment she knew. From some undefined source a sense of peace came to her and prepared her for the news she had to hear.

She chose to accept it in two steps.

"He isn't coming," she said almost calmly.

Tibbs, understanding, shook his head slightly from side to side. "I don't believe so," he said. Then he waited, letting her take her time.

She drew breath and closed her eyes. "He's dead." She stated it as a fact so that the worst would be over. When Tibbs had not spoken for five seconds, she knew it was true.

Still the full realization had not yet come to her. She sensed a feeling of sympathetic understanding in the man who sat quietly nearby. She knew that he wanted to reach out and take her hand to offer her his strength, but that he did not do so because he was conscious of his race—or hers.

When he felt that the time was right, Tibbs spoke again. "I have one more thing to tell you, and it will not be easy to take. Should it be now, or later?"

She looked him squarely in the face. "Now," she said.

He looked back as steadily. "I could be mistaken, but I don't think so. Unless I am wrong, I have to tell you that he was murdered."

Now she understood. "That is why you are here."

Tibbs nodded.

"Do you know who did it?" she asked evenly.

"Not yet," he admitted. "But if you will help me, I'm going to try to find out."

chapter 8

After a short interval Tibbs rose to his feet. "May I use your telephone?" he asked.

After he received nodded permission he picked up the instrument on the counter, dialed, gave his credit-card number, and in a few seconds had Bob Nakamura on the line.

"I have a make," he reported. "I'll get a few details and then come in."

When he had hung up, he turned toward Ellen. "Miss Boardman, I understand how you must feel, and I don't want to intrude on you at this time. It is very important, however, that I talk with you as soon as you feel up to it. You understand why."

Ellen Boardman stared out of the window for a moment, seeing nothing; then, with wet eyes but in control of herself, she looked at Tibbs. "If you could let me have just a few minutes. I want to phone my father so that he can break the news to mother. And I'd like to—think a little bit. After that I'll be glad to do whatever I can."

"Perhaps you'd like to wait until after a formal identification. I might be wrong."

Ellen studied him for a moment. "Are you?" she asked.

It was one of the things a policeman had to do. "I don't think so," he answered. He rose to go.

"Sit down, please. I won't be too long."

"If you don't mind," Tibbs replied, "I'd rather go outside. It's very pleasant up here and I'd enjoy walking around a bit."

As soon as he was gone, Ellen rose tensely and turned toward the telephone. She had to make the call and she wanted it to be over. A few minutes later, she hung up, grateful that the brief ordeal was behind her. She wiped her eyes, replaced the snapshots where they belonged, and glanced at the clock. In ten minutes it would be noon. Relieved that she had something to do, she walked into the small kitchen that served the family and mechanically began the motions of preparing lunch. She set two places.

As she cut a tomato into wedges for the salad, she thought about her Uncle Albert. Now that he was gone, there was little she could do for him. She could pray, and she could help the police, if she was able to, in their search for the person responsible. She did not understand why they had sent a Negro, but then, she reflected, the old differences were disappearing rapidly and perhaps she was just behind the times.

Outside the day was lovely. Somewhere in the neighborhood someone was hammering; it was the sound of life going on, of something being accomplished. . . . She finished the salad and put it on the table.

Ten minutes later she had the lunch ready. She went back to the lobby, but the policeman was not there. She pushed the front door open and saw him; he was standing on the fence railing replacing the sign that had been knocked down. He drove a final nail with the hammer in his hand, jumped down, and put the tool in the trunk of his car.

Ellen walked over to meet him. "That was very nice of you.

You saved me a job, and I'm not very good at that sort of thing."

"You're quite welcome," Tibbs said. "If it's not too much trouble, could I wash?"

"Yes, of course, and then come in for lunch. It's not very much, but we can talk, if you like."

Tibbs followed her in, used the washroom she pointed out, and then joined her in the small dining room. He accepted his lunch without comment and waited until he sensed that she was ready to talk to him.

"If you feel up to it now," he began, "I'd like to ask you some questions about your uncle. Suppose we start with his name."

She nodded. "His name is—was Albert Roussel, *Dr.* Albert Roussel," she added with emphasis.

"He was a physician?"

"No, a chemist. Uncle Albert majored in chemistry at college and was good at it, good enough to earn a scholarship and to go on to his master's. After that he joined a company that encouraged advanced study, and four years later he got his Ph.D."

She thought for a few moments. "He stayed with that company for several years while he did some work on his own at home. His hobby was photography and he worked on the chemistry of films and things like that. After a while he hit on something—" She stopped and shook her head. "I'm getting ahead of the story."

She paused and poured Tibbs a cup of tea. "When my uncle was in college," Ellen went on, "he met a well-known girl, Joyce Bachelor. From what I've been told, I don't think she was a very admirable girl. I gathered that Joyce was for Joyce, and that was all that mattered to her."

She paused, but Tibbs said nothing.

"At the time, Uncle Albert was nevertheless very attracted to her. They went together for some time, during school and afterward. But I gather she felt that the man she married would either have to have or to make a lot of money. I think she liked Uncle Albert—she went with him enough—but she just couldn't see him as a future millionaire, and so that was that."

Telling the story seemed to be relieving her mind. She kept her voice even and almost impersonal.

"Well, she got her way. She did meet a man—an older man —who had the money she wanted, and she married him. At the end of several years he dropped dead on the tennis court one day, and Joyce was left with practically everything. Meanwhile, as I told you, Uncle Albert hit on something—a photographic process of some kind having to do with color. He sold the process on a royalty basis, made a little name for himself, and the money started to flow in."

"And so did Joyce," Tibbs suggested.

"Yes, but not in the way you might think. I'd rather like to think that Uncle Albert told her he wasn't interested any more. By this time he was living in France. Our family on mother's side is of French descent and he spoke the language well. He had a villa there that he liked very much and he said the rural atmosphere of the place helped him in his work.

"I know he was very popular over there; he was such a fine man that he had a host of friends, so Joyce just wasn't in the running any more. At least that's the way I think it was." She paused and took a deep breath. When she went on, her voice had changed in tone. "Anyhow, Joyce had a lot of money now and ideas about making more. So she had an inspiration—to form a holding company to handle Uncle Albert's patents. Maybe she felt he would come up with more if he had additional capital to work with, and she knew where it could be found. So they made a deal."

Ellen stopped as though she had run down; she was on the thin edge of her control.

Tibbs ate very quietly and did nothing to distract her.

Finally she went on, "Three or four people came into the thing and it prospered—on the ideas that Uncle Albert developed, of course. Then he more or less quit. He spent practically all his time in France and only came over here once a year to visit us and to attend a board meeting of the company. Since he was the person who made everything possible, his opinions and ideas were pretty well respected."

"I should think so," Tibbs agreed.

Ellen swallowed hard and then drank some tea. "This year the board meeting seems to be especially important. I don't know the details, but apparently one of the big companies has made an offer to buy out everything. There are only four or five people in the company—Uncle Albert's company, that is —and they have to decide."

"Most of them live locally?" Tibbs asked.

She nodded. "That's right—Joyce and the others. Again, I don't know, but I have the idea that some of them want to sell and others don't. Uncle Albert wrote us that he wanted to be certain he was present this time, though of course he always is anyway."

"How did your uncle feel about the sale?"

Ellen shook her head. "I don't know that. He just wrote that he was definitely coming, that's all."

"He could well have been in a position to hold the balance of power," Tibbs guessed aloud. "In that case, some very strong emotions might have been aroused."

"You mean one of them might have done it?" Ellen asked.

"It's something to look into," Tibbs said.

He drove back to Pasadena with many things on his mind. When he walked into his office, Bob Nakamura was waiting for him. "You've been sold into slavery." he said.

Tibbs sat down behind his desk. "Do I have to address a Boy Scout conclave?"

Bob shook his head. "San Bernardino is delighted that you have identified the body. They were very impressed. Also they added something about what a happy circumstance it was that you were there just when they were shorthanded."

Tibbs looked for a longing moment at the top of his desk. "I have other things to do," he said with a sigh.

"They know, and so does Captain Lindholm. However, officially you are to continue on the case until it is closed. A successful outcome is expected."

Tibbs shook his head. "Why did my mother raise her boy to be a policeman? Why couldn't I just play second base for some nice minor-league team?"

"Because you're not a good enough hitter, I suspect." Bob paused and looked at him sidewise. "Are you enjoying your visits to the nudist camp?"

Tibbs laughed. "It's different, I'll grant you that. Helps to break the monotony. Nice people, though."

"Any pretty girls?"

Tibbs returned the knowing glance. "Wait till you get a

load of Linda. Also you might try sitting across from people who are comfortably undressed—completely, that is—and who ask you how you like police work."

"I think I might just enjoy that," Bob mused. "When I married Amiko, I accepted certain restrictions, of course, but I wasn't struck blind."

"I'll get you an application," Tibbs offered generously. "They already have several Nisei members—they told me."

"I don't think Amiko would go for it. Though personally I wouldn't mind," Bob said. "Some of my best friends are Caucasians."

Calmly Virgil picked up his phone and dialed both area code and number from memory. After the normal amount of clicking and three audible rings, Linda's voice came on the line.

"Good afternoon, Linda," Tibbs said, carefully underlining her name. "This is Virgil."

Without hesitation Bob Nakamura picked up his phone and pushed the button that would put him on the line.

"Why, hello, Virgil!" he heard her say. "Are you coming in?"

"Not today, but I called to let you and your family know that we have identified the body found in your pool."

"Please—who was he?"

"I'm sure you didn't even know of him. He was an American scientist who was living in France."

"You were right!" she exclaimed over the line. "Everything you said was true. I don't know about the swimming part, but I bet you were right there, too."

Tibbs noted with mild disapproval that Bob had elected to listen in.

"Linda, how is the weather out there?" he asked.

"Beautiful. I just came out of the water. I'm on the poolside extension now. Come and take a swim."

Bob puckered his lips and looked toward the ceiling.

"Thank you for inviting me. And when you get back to the house, I'd like to ask you to do me a favor," Tibbs went on smoothly. "A close friend of mine would like an application for membership. A Mr. Robert Nakamura. Would you send him one in care of the Pasadena Police Department?"

"Is he a single?" Linda asked.

"No, he has a lovely wife; you'll like her." Tibbs' face showed no sign of emotion. "And a son six, a daughter four."

"That's fine, Virgil. If they're friends of yours, then I know we would like to have them. I'll send you an application, too."

Recognizing instantly that he was being flanked, Tibbs said a quick "Thank you" and hung up. "You're in," he said to Bob with pleasant candor.

"So are you."

Tibbs shook his head. "I don't think so. They don't accept singles; you heard her. And besides—" He stopped.

The frivolity was gone.

Bob picked his words carefully. "She invited you. You didn't even have to ask. And she called you Virgil."

"They call everybody by his first name," Tibbs explained, almost too quickly. "It's a custom they have."

On the way to Beverly Hills and on through to Bel Air, Tibbs was annoyed with himself. Linda had pulled his leg, just as he had been pulling hers. But regardless of her friendliness, and that of her family, he felt that it was one more place closed to him because of his background. The neighbors had apparently accepted the nudist park well enough, but what would their attitude be if they spotted Negro members going in and out of the gate? He remembered the applicant he had encountered on his first visit. If a Negro family were to join the club, how many others would resign in protest? There would be some, he felt sure of that.

He consulted the address slip clipped to the hot sheet and then turned in through an ornate gateway to the exclusive residential area. The winding roadway climbed slowly up toward the foothills of the Santa Monica Mountains, passing the elaborate mansions of the movie colony and the owners of electronics plants. Sprinkled along the curb were the neat compact trucks of the Japanese-American gardeners who maintained the carefully combed appearance of the lawns and shrubbery.

The residence of Mrs. Joyce Bachelor Pratt was a little smaller than some of its neighbors, which put it somewhere in the eighty- to one-hundred-thousand-dollar bracket. An asphalt driveway led uphill to a three-car garage and a small parking area beside the house. For a moment Tibbs contemplated leaving his car at the curb and walking the rest of the way; then he decided to drive in, as any other visitor would do.

He ignored the sign that pointed the way to the rear entrance, and pressed the button at the front door. A Negro maid answered; when she saw Tibbs, her face broke into a pleasant smile. "Yes, sir?" she inquired.

Tibbs offered his calling card. The maid glanced at it, lifted her eyebrows slightly, and opened the door wider. "Please come in, sir," she said. As Tibbs stepped inside, she added, "I'll see if Mrs. Pratt is at home."

She disappeared with the card; as she walked away Tibbs noted with approval that she kept her hips still and her body straight.

Presently he heard voices from another room. He caught the words "This gentleman is calling to see you, Madam."

He was fully prepared for Mrs. Pratt to be an impressive woman, not necessarily large, but somewhat in the *grande-dame* style. When she appeared, he was reminded again never to jump to conclusions. She was very small, just touching five feet, and slender enough to suggest that she did not weigh much over a hundred pounds. He had expected her to be fifty, which she obviously was despite considerable effort on her part to halt the progress of time. There was about her mouth and still-dimpled chin a certain kittenishness and the hint of a seductive pout. In her youth she had clearly been the little warm thing who was fragile, "cute," and who offered sex potential in a compact package. Her hair was light and had been cut just short enough to frame the small features of her face.

When she saw Tibbs, she stopped dead and the half smile that had curved her mouth disappeared. "You wished to see me?" she asked, and let a trace of emphasis linger on the first word.

"Good morning, Mrs. Pratt. Yes, I would—officially."

Joyce Pratt wrinkled her small brow and looked at his card once more. "I haven't been in Pasadena for almost two months," she protested.

The maid, who was standing behind her, watched Tibbs intently.

"This concerns you only indirectly, Mrs. Pratt," he told her. "But it is necessary for me to ask you a few questions."

The maid stepped back to enable her to invite him in.

Mrs. Pratt took her time. "Did you want to come in?" she asked in a tone that clearly suggested a negative answer.

"Thank you," Tibbs replied, and walked in. He found himself in a living room that was half boudoir; the furniture was extremely feminine as were the many varicolored pillows scattered about and the curtains that spanned the wide windows. The painstakingly created atmosphere told him a lot about the owner and why the big man who lay in the morgue in San Bernardino had found her attractive. Her petite size and her apparent need for protection had been, and were, her stock in trade.

He turned and waited until his hostess had reluctantly followed him in. When at last she sank into a chair with studied care, he chose one end of an astonishingly soft davenport, where he could be near enough to talk easily but still far enough away to avoid any familiarity.

"Mrs. Pratt," he began, "I understand you are a close friend of Dr. Albert Roussel's, and a stockholder in the company that markets his patents."

There was no femininity in her voice when she answered him; her tone was cold and sapphire hard. "I do not care to discuss Dr. Roussel. If you want to know anything about him, I suggest that you speak to him personally, if he will see you. Will that be all?"

Tibbs pushed his fingers together to give her time to understand he was not that easily dismissed. "Mrs. Pratt," he said presently, "I dislike very much to bring you distressing news, but it may not be possible to do that."

She looked sharply at him. "What do you mean?" She

snapped the words out, hard and brittle, as though she would not allow him to tell her such a thing.

"Mrs. Pratt," Tibbs spoke very slowly. "I greatly regret to inform you that a man closely answering Dr. Roussel's description was found dead a few days ago. Although there has been no formal identification as yet, we believe it to be him."

"*Not* the body in the nudist colony!" She almost barked the words and then pointed with obvious distaste to the morning paper that lay folded on a table.

"That is the man."

"It's outrageous."

Tibbs nodded in agreement. "Murder usually is."

They were interrupted by the maid, who appeared pushing in a mahogany cart that held an exquisite Japanese tea service on its glass top. She advanced quietly into the room and stopped beside her mistress.

Joyce Pratt turned and looked at her. "What is that for?" she demanded.

"You instructed me to prepare tea for all guests, Madam," the maid said.

"This man is not a guest."

The maid backed the teacart, swung it around, and left the room without looking at either of the occupants.

Virgil Tibbs took out his notebook and became formally official. "Mrs. Pratt, how many stockholders are there in your holding company, including the deceased?"

"Is it necessary for me to discuss this with you?"

Tibbs had had about enough. If Joyce Pratt thought that all he had to do was sit there all day and allow her to insult him, she had another guess coming. He did not change the tone of his voice, but there was an edge to his words that could not be mistaken. "No, it is not necessary. If you prefer, I will arrest you as a material witness and take you to jail. Then you can discuss the matter with your attorney and the prosecuting authorities." He gambled that she was not familiar with legal processes and matters of jurisdiction.

He won; he watched her as she wilted. "Five stockholders," she said a little weakly. "That's including Albert."

"I believe you organized the company?"

"Well—more or less. I have many well-to-do friends, of course, and because I thought it was a good thing, I told some of them about it. They agreed with me after looking into it and they bought stock."

"Was the venture fully successful?"

She replied by waving her arm to indicate the whole room.

"Are you the business manager of the company?"

"No. Walter McCormack does that. He has much more experience in the field and, of course, he's a lot older. Would you—would you care for some tea?"

"No, thank you. And the others?" Tibbs was busy with his notebook.

"William Holt-Rymers." He thought he detected the suggestion of a sniff in that. "Oswald Peterson."

Tibbs looked up. "The football player?"

"Oh, do you know him?"

"Only by reputation. One of the stars of the professional game, I believe."

"Not any more. He used to be, but he isn't any more."

Tibbs asked a number of further questions, which brought out the fact that the holding company, a small, tight one, had been a prime investment. "What about Dr. Roussel's own interest?" he asked finally. "His family is abroad?"

Joyce shook her head. "No, Albert never married. I think he was shy with most women—although he never was with me. He had charm—great charm—and of course the women were attracted to him. Naturally. He would have been a great catch for anyone. But he was always reserved somehow. . . ."

He wondered how much she was reflecting her own mind. "His stock?" he reminded her.

"Oh, yes, his stock. Well, it was part of our agreement that no one can sell his shares without offering them to the others first. Of course that wouldn't pertain to inheritances."

"Do you have any information as to who might be Dr. Roussel's heir?"

Joyce looked at him narrowly. "His only close relatives were his sister, her husband, I suppose, and there is a niece." She reached down and smoothed her skirt to suggest a modesty that her next words contradicted. "You'll probably find this out anyway, so I might as well tell you. Albert was terribly broken up when I married someone else. Everyone knew it. That's why he never married—he told me so. And, of course, I am the person who financed and made possible his success."

"What you are saying, Mrs. Pratt, is that you felt he may have left some of his holdings to you?"

"I have no doubt of it, and I don't think that his sister does, either. Quite frankly I am the girl he wanted, and besides that, as I told you, I brought him his success."

"And his interest in you has remained—through the years."

Joyce lifted her head and faced him confidently; when she spoke, her voice was calm and controlled. "On that I can be quite definite," she answered. "In fact everything had been planned. After Albert's usual visit with his sister and after the board meeting, we were going to France together. Then we were to have been married there, two months from today."

chapter 9

The following morning Ellen Boardman chose a simple white dress, which her Uncle Albert had admired, for the unpleasant duty she had to perform. Because the day was very hot, and the sun blazed sharply in the sky, she also wore a cartwheel hat. As she gave her hair a final pat to adjust it into place, she also tried to attune her mind to the idea that she was going to be in the company of a Negro.

If she had been asked, she would have said that she was free of prejudice. And she would have meant it. However, until the moment that Virgil Tibbs had walked in the front door of Pine Shadows Lodge, she had never had any real contact with Negro people. She had talked to many working in various jobs, but it had always been on a different basis. Of course this was not a social engagement she was going on—far from it—but it would be the first time she had ever been escorted by anyone not of her own color. She looked again into the mirror and touched up her lipstick.

When Virgil Tibbs drove up—on time almost to the minute—she met him at the door. He paused for a second to look at her, with admiration, but without any hint of familiarity. Then he greeted her—a little stiffly, she thought. "Good morning, Miss Boardman. I'm so glad it's such a nice day."

"So am I," she replied.

He helped her into the car; for a moment she wondered if he would open the rear door for her, but he did not. As he slid behind the wheel and started the engine, she tried to evaluate him once more. He was certainly neat; his summer-weight suit was well cut and had come from a good shop. Though he had already had a long, hot drive, his white shirt was fresh and immaculate. While he drove, she studied his profile and decided that he was a good-looking man.

Tibbs glanced at her and misread her thoughts. "Miss Boardman, I know how you must feel about the duty ahead of you, but try to put it out of your mind. What happened is all over now—finished and done with. It may help you to think of it that way."

She did find the thought comforting. "It was very kind of you to come and drive me," she said.

"I'm happy to," Virgil answered. He swung the car with expert skill around a curve, moved the automatic transmission into a lower range, and started down the long grade.

In a quiet way the magic of the near-perfect day began to work its familiar miracle to the point where Ellen found herself in an almost relaxed frame of mind. When they reached the bend at the bottom of the first long slope, she indicated the broad turnout where the view of the valley below is at its most spectacular. "That's my favorite spot," she said. "I never come past here without stopping for a few minutes."

In response Tibbs swung the car off the blacktop and onto the gravel.

"I'm sorry. I didn't mean that I wanted to stop now," she apologized. "Perhaps when we come back."

Virgil nodded. "Let's do it that way." He turned the car smoothly back onto the two-lane road.

Half an hour later, in the city, Tibbs guided the car expertly through the traffic and pulled up outside the morgue. There he helped Ellen out and escorted her quietly into the building. Though the attendants were kind with her, she was grateful for Tibbs' presence when she was taken into the grim room where she would have to make the identification. She looked at the still face of death for a moment, closed her eyes bitterly against the sight, and nodded her head.

Quickly she was taken outside and given a form with which to claim the body. It was a coroner's case, which complicated the legal situation, and several things had to be done. When the formalities were over, Ellen borrowed the telephone and called a funeral home with which she had already made tentative arrangements. She made a second call to her minister and then turned to Tibbs.' "Could we go now?" she asked. "And I'd like to talk to you for a few minutes, if I may."

"Of course." He took her back to the car, moved it out into traffic, and headed back toward the mountain-resort area.

"Mr. Tibbs," she said when they had driven a short distance. "Please tell me the truth. I've been wondering—why was my uncle found on the grounds of—of that awful place?"

"I don't know," Tibbs answered truthfully.

"Was he a—patron there?"

"No, he wasn't. I'm sure of that."

'I don't know what kind of people could run a place like that," she said, a little bitterly. "There must be something basically wrong with them."

"Without holding any brief for their line of business," Virgil answered her, "I'd say they're considerably better than average people. I'm prejudiced, I admit, because they ignored my color."

She was startled to hear him speak of it so factually.

"Do you want to know something else?" Tibbs asked.

"Please."

"When they discovered your uncle, they immediately did everything possible to revive him. That included mouth-to-mouth respiration, which isn't pleasant for anyone—under the circumstances. If there had been a spark of life left, I think they would have brought him around. They certainly tried."

"I didn't know that," Ellen said.

"They have a son, George, who has had life-guard training. He pulled your uncle out of the pool and did exactly the right things until the rescue units and the doctor got there. He was sure there was no hope, but they kept at it until the doctor made it definite."

"I'll write and thank them," she said.

Tibbs pulled up at the curb beside an attractive-looking drive-in. "How about some coffee or something? This *hasn't* been pleasant for you. Let me go and get you something."

She realized he was trying to distract her, to make things easier. And that he had chosen this place so he wouldn't compel her to accept his company in public. "Can't we go inside?" she suggested.

She was proud of herself for her decision—still proud as she drank the milk shake she had chosen and he had bought for her. She saw the bold stares of a pair of long-haired teen-agers in the next booth and returned them calmly.

"Hey, Joe, you know what's got three eyes, four legs, and is black and white?" The voice from the next booth was deliberately loud and Ellen knew it was.

"O.K., what is?" insolently.

"Mr. and Mrs. Sammy Davis, Jr."

She looked at Tibbs. He shrugged his shoulders, then excused himself to go to the phone. She waited for him, her chin in the air.

As soon as Tibbs returned. they went outside and she paused for a moment on the sidewalk. She took a deep breath. "May I impose on you a great deal?" she asked. "Much more than I have already?"

"Of course, Miss Boardman. What would you like?"

"How far is it to the nudist colony?"

He answered by opening the car door and helping her inside. They had gone several blocks before she could think of anything further she wanted to say. "Have you any clues at all as to whom . . . who might be guilty of my uncle's death?"

"Yes, but I'm afraid I can't discuss it with you," Virgil replied. "You can understand why."

She bit her lip and said, "Yes, I guess so. This is really a terrible imposition on you, taking me to see these people."

"Not at all. It's more or less on the way."

"Perhaps we ought to stop somewhere and tell them we're coming." A sudden violent thought hit her. "I won't have to—" She was unable to say the words. The idea of taking all her clothes off, probably in front of strange men, was paralyzing. "I couldn't!" she added, knowing he would understand.

"They won't expect it of you," Tibbs assured her. "Otherwise I wouldn't put myself in the position of taking you. They are really nice people; I believe you'll like them."

"I do already for having tried the way they did to save Uncle Albert's life, even though they couldn't. But shouldn't we let them know we're coming?"

"I've already done that, from the restaurant."

"Oh." She remembered that he had gone to the phone, but that was *before* she had asked him to take her to see these people. She decided that he really was a detective and that she'd better be a little more guarded when she was in his presence. She rode on quietly until she felt the car slowing and saw the sign for Sun Valley Lodge that had been reproduced in the newspapers.

Virgil drove in past the intentional turns in the entrance road and pulled up on the parking lot. Remembering his own experience with Linda the last time he had seen her, he turned toward Ellen. "You understand that the people here will probably not be dressed." That was an understatement; on such a fine day it was practically a certainty.

"I'm prepared," Ellen answered. He looked carefully at her face and decided that she would take it in her stride.

He was watching Ellen so intently that he did not hear Linda as she approached across the grass; he was first aware of her when she spoke a warm "Hello, Virgil" practically in his ear. He turned quickly and for the first time in his life was shocked to discover that he was looking at a fully clothed young woman.

Linda had on a smart yellow frock that set off her good looks to perfection. Her hair was neatly arranged and she had used a small amount of lipstick with rewarding effect. Only her sandaled feet were a concession to informality.

He recovered himself and introduced Ellen. "I know," Linda said simply. "Please come in, we're expecting you. Virgil phoned."

As Ellen got out of the car, she reflected that the only shock so far was hearing her quietly dignified escort called by his first name. On the way to the main house, Forrest

Nunn met them in a sport shirt and slacks. In honor of the occasion George had elected to wear a white shirt and a tie so that he looked the part of the rising young man to perfection.

Tibbs watched with interest as the Nunns made Ellen welcome, extended her their sympathy, and within five minutes had her sitting, relaxed and contented, with a tall glass of iced tea and a piece of homemade cake before her. Soon Ellen was telling them about her uncle, the strain had left her face, and she seemed to accept the fact that she was among friends. After about half an hour, George drew Tibbs aside.

"Virgil, what happens when you and Miss Boardman leave here?" he asked.

Allowing himself a moment of quiet amusement but keeping a straight face, Virgil replied, "I'm going to take Miss Boardman home. Then it's back to Pasadena and whatever is waiting for me there."

"That's a lot of driving," George suggested.

"I'm used to it."

George said thoughtfully, "Ellen, on short acquaintance, seems like an exceptionally nice girl."

Virgil nodded slowly. "I agree."

"Are you interested—personally?"

Tibbs appreciated that. He said, "No, definitely not. For several reasons, one of them being that she is concerned in a case that I am investigating."

Each man fully understood the other. And each knew that a thread of friendship had been spun between them.

"Then how would it be with you if I offered to take Ellen home? Assuming that it's all right with her, of course."

"Why don't you ask her?" It was a considered decision;

technically Ellen Boardman was his responsibility, and George was not yet cleared of possible connection with the crime, even though he had raised the alarm and used first-aid techniques. He was an able-bodied male known to have been on the scene. However, the risk involved in an assault on Ellen Boardman under the circumstances would have been suicidal, and Tibbs, fully aware of this, allowed George to go ahead.

A few minutes later George asked her, and Ellen showed her own intelligence by glancing quickly at Tibbs for a cue.

Virgil said, "If it's agreeable with you, Miss Boardman, go ahead. It will give me a chance to get back to my office and attend to some rather pressing matters. But if you'd like to continue our discussion, then I'd be very happy to run you on up."

"You have been extremely kind to me," she said. "By all means, go ahead. And thank you very much—for everything."

As Tibbs rose to go, Linda volunteered to go with him to the parking lot.

"I like Ellen," the girl said as they walked. "And I think George does, too."

"I would say that was fairly obvious," Virgil responded.

"Do you have a girl, Virgil?"

"I have some friends, of course. No one that I'm serious about—at least not yet."

"After this is all over and you have caught the murderer, will you come back and see us? We'd like you to."

Tibbs stopped by his car and took his time getting in behind the wheel. "I'd like to very much," he said finally. "I like your family and this is a very pleasant place. But there are obstacles, as you realize. In the first place, I'm not a nudist, and forgive me if I add that I have no immediate plans to become one." He fitted the key into the lock. "Then, too, Linda, we do represent different segments of humanity."

She rested her hands on the window sill of the car. "You know how we all feel about that," she said.

"I do and I'm extremely grateful for it. I was in the Deep South a few weeks ago on a case down there. It was quite different."

"It doesn't affect your work, does it? I mean, representing a different segment of humanity."

"There are some annoyances, but not among my colleagues. There has been a lot of progress in the last few years. Have you ever had to take it on the chin from someone because you were a nudist?"

"For a while, yes, when I was in school. Not so much any more. People are learning."

"I agree, they are."

"We're going to have a dance here in a little while," Linda said. "An evening affair—clothed, of course. We'd all be very pleased if you'd come."

"Possibly," Tibbs answered. "On the condition that I could bring my own date. You understand, don't you?"

"Yes, Virgil, I understand. If you come, will you ask me for a dance?"

"If it's customary here, Linda, yes, I would be very happy to. In some places I wouldn't, because that would be—" He was at a loss for the right word.

"Premature?" Linda suggested.

"Thank you. As you wouldn't appear undressed on the streets of San Bernardino, would you?"

"Certainly not!"

"Yet we might live to see the day when it will be quite

customary on the beaches, the way things are going."

"I'm sure of it," Linda agreed. "But I understand what you mean. I'll make a date with you. Let's agree to celebrate the twenty-fourth or twenty-fifth anniversary of the date that you catch the murderer. Things ought to be different then."

"Of course they will be. You'll undoubtedly be married, for one thing. Perhaps I will be, too."

"Well, I should hope so. Goodbye, Virgil."

"Goodbye, Linda." He backed the car around, and drove out onto the highway.

chapter 10

The telephone of Walter McCormack, the millionaire business manager of Roussel Rights, Inc., was not listed, so Tibbs had to spend a few extra minutes before he had the residence of the millionaire on the line. When he did get through, the person who answered was not cooperative.

"Mr. McCormack is not available to see anyone," he was informed.

"Perhaps I didn't make myself clear," Virgil replied patiently. "I'm speaking officially, as a police officer. I have under investigation a very serious matter in which Mr. McCormack is at least indirectly involved. It is essential that I see him as soon as possible."

If his words had any effect, the results were not apparent. "Mr. McCormack is not available. If there are legal problems involved, I suggest that you call his attorney, Mr. Michael Wolfram." The line went dead.

His temper rising, Tibbs checked the directory again and called the attorney's office. Being turned down on a request for an official interview was almost unheard of, particularly by people who might be under suspicion. When the telephone receptionist answered Wolfram's line, Tibbs was unintentionally short with her. In a few seconds he had the attorney on the other end and explained his problem.

"Mr. Tibbs, the same thing happens to everyone. Please don't take personal offense," Wolfram explained. "Mr. Mc-Cormack is an extremely reserved person and usually makes his own rules. He prefers to see no one and that's the way it is. I spend a good deal of my time placating people who have had the same experience as you had. If you call personally at his residence, he might see you, but I rather seriously doubt it."

"How would you suggest I arrange to see him?" Tibbs asked. "I must do so as soon as possible."

"You might write him a letter. He reads his mail and then does whatever he thinks best. I'd allow a week, though. Mr. McCormack doesn't like to be rushed into anything."

"As his attorney, could you call him and point out the need to see me now?"

"Mr. Tibbs, please understand that it wouldn't be of any use. He has given definite instructions on the point. I believe a letter would be your best solution."

His temper now thoroughly aroused, Tibbs left the office and pointed his car westward toward Malibu. It was a long drive, and he had to watch himself in the hurrying freeway traffic not to let his irritation upset his judgment. To change his outlook, he turned on the radio and listened to a play-by-play of the California Angels, who were having a good one with the Yankees. By the time he reached the Pacific shoreline, he had regained his usual composure.

The residence of Walter McCormack was set well back and heavily screened by shrubbery. At the entrance there was a sign that unnecessarily read "PRIVATE"; heavy metal gates made it clear that casual visitors were not wanted. Virgil parked his car, walked up to the small uninviting pedestrian entryway, and let himself in.

Once on the grounds he admitted to himself that the seclusion was pleasant. As the terrain rose, a view of the ocean was unfolded and the cool air off the water had a refreshing saltiness. The huge lawn, which was beautifully kept, surrounded a big half-timbered English manor house that reigned with patrician dignity. It was the kind of home no policeman could ever hope to have.

As Tibbs approached the house up the wide driveway, he saw a sizeable Negro in blue coveralls who was washing a black Cadillac with a garden hose and a large soft sponge. The man looked up as Virgil came closer and stopped his work for a moment to observe him. Tibbs continued up the driveway until he was within speaking range.

"Is Mr. McCormack in?" he asked. The big car suggested he was, but the question served a purpose.

The chauffeur looked at him in surprise. "There's no work to be had here. McCormack gets anybody he needs through an agency."

"I'm not after work," Virgil answered. He took out a small leather case and displayed his shield.

The chauffeur looked at the shield and whistled softly. "Trouble?" he asked.

"Maybe not, but I've got to see Mr. McCormack. What's the best way?"

The big man shook his head slowly. "There just ain't no best way. Mr. McCormack is a real tough man. Lots of people try to see him, but he doesn't see nobody."

"Has he an office?"

"No office—he don't need one. He's got all the money he needs. All he wants to do is stay here and enjoy himself."

Tibbs looked again at the long rolling vista of the ocean. "I can't blame him for that," he said. "But I've got to see him just the same."

Eloquently the chauffeur lifted his shoulders and let them fall. Then he directed the water from the hose back onto the side of the car and began to wipe slowly, dividing his interest between his work and the conversation in progress. "Don't bother to ring the front doorbell. It won't do you no good."

"Somebody should answer," Tibbs said reasonably.

"Maybe, but you won't get in—not even with that badge you got. I know. The orders are to let no one in, no matter who. Anybody who lets anyone in gets fired, right then. So if you make 'em let you in, somebody loses his job."

"What's your name?" Tibbs asked.

"I'm Brown—Walter Brown. The boss don't like it I've got the same name he has, so he calls me Brown all the time. He wanted me to change it once, and offered to have his lawyer fix it up. I told him I liked it the way it was."

"Good for you." Tibbs thought a minute and decided to leave and take a different tack. "I'll see you later."

To Virgil's surprise the chauffeur put down his tools to walk him part way back to the front gate. "If you need any more help," he offered, "let me know."

Tibbs thanked him and handed him his card. "I'm going to try to get invited to see Mr. McCormack. If you happen to see him yourself and can do so, I'd appreciate your telling him personally that a police officer has been trying to reach him concerning an important matter."

Brown accepted the card and tucked it carefully away in an inner pocket. "Now wouldn't exactly be the time to do that. He's been pretty upset lately. You read the papers?"

Tibbs nodded.

Brown dropped his voice a shade, although there was no one to overhear him. "One of his good friends got himself killed in a nudist camp and he didn't like that one bit. Enough so now he won't even see his lawyer. Mr. Wolfram is different; he can usually get in any time."

"Any time?" Tibbs inquired.

"That's right, night or day."

"Does anyone else have that privilege?"

Brown shook his head. "Nope. Mr. Wolfram's the only one."

"Is there a Mrs. McCormack?"

"There was, but she's been dead a long time. A real nice lady, too."

Tibbs digested this information during lunch and then drove down the coast highway. In order to relax as much as he could, he stayed in the right-hand lane, where he could take in the sweeping vastness of the water and let it work its unhurried magic on his spirit. When he felt that he had indulged in his reverie long enough, he reminded himself firmly of the job he had in hand and pulled up at a roadside telephone. The number of William Holt-Rymers, one of the four surviving stockholders of the Roussel holding company, was listed in Venice. Virgil dialed.

The phone was answered almost immediately. "Bill Rymers," said a voice that was brisk but without harshness. It was a statement of fact.

Tibbs introduced himself and asked for an appointment.

"Where are you now?" Holt-Rymers asked.

Tibbs told him.

"Come on down—it's an easy place to find. Be sure you turn off before Pacific Ocean Park. If you get there, you've gone too far."

Virgil got back into his car and continued southward. He drove through Santa Monica and entered the less impressive Venice area, checking the street numbers as he went along.

A mile short of the amusement park he found the place he wanted; it was close to the ocean, fairly small, and wedged in between two other equally weather-beaten structures typical of close-to-the-beach property rented out on a weekly basis to summer visitors. The ancient wooden clapboards had been painted gray at some time in the past, as had all the other substandard buildings on the short block; now they had resigned themselves to the colorless hue bestowed upon them by sun, wind, and salt water. Virgil checked the number carefully and got out of his car.

The man who opened the door gave an immediate impression of height, leanness, and casual physical discipline. He was somewhere in his mid-thirties, his face partly hidden by a short beard that suggested a jazz musician. Tibbs guessed him as about six feet, although he appeared taller because of his bare torso, which was tightly muscled and deeply browned by the sun. He wore Bermuda shorts and a pair of indifferent leather sandals, and a towel lay across his shoulders as though he had just come from a plunge in a nearby swimming pool.

"Tibbs?" he asked without ceremony. Before Virgil could answer, he shook hands briefly and firmly, and then stepped aside to let his guest enter; total informality surrounded him and infused the room he stood in. The furniture was plain, worn, but basic—the selections of a man who knew his own mind. The walls were vivid, in four different colors, which managed amazingly to achieve a look of harmony. The available light came though partially shuttered windows and formed angular shadows on the surfaces where it struck. Stuck about the walls were three unframed prints of works by Gauguin and several oil canvases whose virgin-white edges contrasted violently with the brilliant pigments of the wall surfaces. The whole effect was totally uninhibited, masculine, and doubtless matched the owner.

Holt-Rymers motioned his guest to a chair and said "Beer?" making the word an inquiry, a suggestion, and a commentary on the hot day.

Virgil knew better than to give a stiff answer to this man about being on duty. "Cold," he said.

His host gave him a quick glance of approval and opened a refrigerator that stood in one corner of the room. Removing two cans, he popped the lids and handed one of the cans to Virgil. Then he settled himself into a chair and stretched out his long legs in an attitude of complete relaxation. "Begin," he invited.

Since the conversation had so far consisted entirely of one-word speeches, Virgil was tempted to say "Murder," just to see what the reaction would be. Instead he took a cooling drink and then started in a low key. "This concerns a business associate of yours, I believe—Dr. Albert Roussel."

Holt-Rymers leaned back in his chair and pressed his lips together for a moment. "Al Roussel—one of the best," he said. He let the obituary hang in the air for a few moments and then came back to the present. "Forgive me," he went on. "It hit me hard when I heard it. I still don't believe it. I'd read about the body in the nudist camp, of course—everybody has, I think. But it never occurred to me that it could be anyone I know. You just don't think of things that way. Then, not more than ten minutes ago, I caught the newsflash."

He stopped and drank from his beer can.

"You knew he was murdered?" Tibbs asked.

"I guess so. Of course I did. I just hadn't connected Al with the anonymous body. I'm still confused, I guess. It wasn't even in the morning paper. What I can't figure out is why anyone would want to do in as fine a fellow as Al. He didn't have an enemy in the world."

"He had one."

"Yes, obviously, but I can't bring myself to believe it."

"How well did you know him?" Virgil asked.

"Very well. Perhaps I'd better fill you in. Do you know my line?"

Tibbs nodded toward the opposite wall. "If those paintings are yours, then you're an artist."

Holt-Rymers nodded. "Nicely put, and thank you. You're right, I paint. Apparently to some purpose, because my stuff sells. Well enough so that I have a waiting list at the dealer who handles me. On the average, I do six canvases a year at around three thousand per, net to me, for the commercial market. The rest of the time I do what I please, paint what I like, and live here because I want to."

He stopped for another few swallows of beer, leaned back, and went on, "Painting is like anything else. If you want to be any good at it, you have to learn how. I spent several years in Europe studying techniques, materials, and the rudiments of style."

"Excuse me," Virgil interrupted, "but have you ever sold any of your work to Walter McCormack?"

"Yes, he has a seascape of mine over his mantelpiece, but

that isn't how we met, if that's what you're getting at."

"Sorry. Please go on." As he drank from his own can, he realized how quickly his host had followed his logic.

"While I was in Paris learning my trade, I ran into Al Roussel. That was some time ago, before he made his pile. We had a lot in common, including the wish to live our own lives, and we got to be good friends. More beer?"

"I'm still good, thanks."

"After we really got to know each other, Al told me about a new film process he had just worked out and that he thought might make a fair amount of money. When he explained to me what it would do, I agreed with him. He had some money in those days, but not a great deal, so we made a bargain. I had the luck to sell a couple of pieces and invested the money in Al's venture. If it panned out, fine. If not, then all I was out was a couple of pictures."

"That was a generous way of looking at it," Tibbs said.

"There's no such thing as success without risk. Well, as you know, Al came through and my little investment in him paid off handsomely. A woman he had known for some time put up some more capital, and a holding company was formed. It was largely four people: Al, Walter McCormack, a fellow named Ozzie Peterson who had made quite a bit playing professional football, and the woman—Joyce Pratt. Have you met her?"

"Yes," Tibbs answered.

"She was the moving spirit and more or less ran things, with McCormack as the actual business manager. Then Al tossed in the golden apple:—he put it that since I had invested money in his work early in the game when no one else would take a chance on him, I would have to be an equal partner in the deal. That upset little Joyce a lot. As an artist, I had no social standing, of course, and my modest investment was peanuts compared to all the others. However, Al made it stick and I got a full fifth of the company. After that I could paint without having to worry where the beer and skittles were coming from. Now that I'm hung in a few museums here and there and the price of my stuff keeps going up on the market, Joyce has more or less accepted me as an endurable evil."

"Now there's a deal on to sell the company."

"Yes."

"A good one?"

"No. Even with Al gone, the assets will grow in value. The patents Al left us are basic, and aren't likely to be outdated for a long time."

"Do you know how Joyce feels?"

"She's money-hungry and wants to sell. Since her husband died, she has no more coming in from that source and she wants all she can get right now."

"McCormack?"

"I don't really know, but he's pretty cagey and I would guess he'd like to hang on."

"How about Peterson?"

"My guess is he would like to sell."

"So it looks like two and two, then, with Dr. Roussel, up to the time of his death, holding the balance of power."

"As I see it, yes."

"Do you know what his feelings were on the matter?" Tibbs drank the remainder of his beer, which had lost its chill and was a little flat.

"Not definitely, but I'm pretty sure he was for hanging on.

He knew his stuff was good and he had more coming up. The man was a genius in his field."

"Did you see him any time during this last visit?"

"No, as a matter of fact, I was out of town."

"Where?"

"Out in the desert by myself—painting."

Tibbs decided, for his own reasons, on an abrupt change of subject. "I want to see Walter McCormack," he said.

"And he won't let you in," Holt-Rymers said.

"Out at his place I was told that if anyone admitted me, he would be fired on the spot."

"Probably true. McCormack is a stiff-necked old buzzard who still believes in the ruling aristocracy, of which he has elected himself a life member. Decent enough in his way, but to him a servant is a thing—a chattel. So are the citizens of the republic, with the exception of the few who travel in his circle."

"How do you stand with him?"

"Strangely, he accepts me. In his opinion my pictures raise me above the masses because he happens to like them. I'm not considered to be on his level, of course, but I'm like Beethoven—allowed to live under the roof."

"Can you get me in to see him?"

"I doubt it. Don't misunderstand me—I'd be glad to try, but my tolerance doesn't extend beyond myself."

Tibbs laced his fingers together. "I'd like to ask a favor of you," he said. "I'd like a three-day option to buy your stock in the holding company. I know you have an agreement and that I can't exercise it. Also I don't have that kind of money."

Holt-Rymers got up from his chair, went to the refrigerator, and came back with two more beers. He handed one to Virgil, took a swallow of his own, and then asked, "As a lever to get in to see McCormack?"

"If I had the option, he might invite me over—just to tell me I can't use it," Virgil added.

"You might make him mad."

"Then we'd be even. He irritated me."

Holt-Rymers took a moment to think. "I'll trade you," he said after drinking more beer. "You get the option, provided you give me a proper safeguard against its use, if you'll do a favor for me."

"Traffic ticket?" Tibbs asked.

The artist looked at him. "You call that a trade? No, something else entirely. I want you to introduce me at the nudist camp—that is, if you've been there and know the people."

"I've been there, all right, but you don't need me for that."

"In a way I do." Holt-Rymers tipped back his head and drank deeply from the can. "Suppose I hire a model and she reports to me here. I put her on a stand and go to work, but what kind of feeling do I get? Closed in, restricted—with the shutters down to keep people from peeking in while I'm at work. Results—one bad picture. If I could arrange with the nudist-camp people to paint there occasionally, it could make all the difference. I'd provide my own model, but if there are people out there who might be willing to work for me for a fee, so much the better. With real outdoor light and space around me, I could create some things worth looking at. Do you think they would go for it?"

Virgil reflected on it for a few seconds. "I'll give it a try," he offered. "They are intelligent, reasonable people and I think they'll buy it. And I can think of one possible subject for you—their daughter. About eighteen and quite attractive. You might even call her beautiful."

Holt-Rymers pointed to the telephone. Virgil crossed the room, and picked up the phone. When Forrest answered, he outlined the proposition, listened, and waited while Linda was consulted. After five minutes on the line he hung up and, with a sense of satisfaction, turned back to his host.

"You're in," he announced.

The artist got to his feet. "Give me a couple of minutes to get dressed; then we can go over to the bank building and have the option drawn up in proper legal style. That will give you something to show McCormack, and he'll want to see it. How do you plan to convince him that you can afford to buy in?"

"By keeping my mouth shut. If I act as though I have the money, it will be up to him to challenge it."

"I'd give a lot to be there," Holt-Rymers said as he left the room.

chapter 11

The office of O. W. Peterson, investment securities, was in Beverly Hills; as he drove there, Tibbs allowed himself a little self-satisfaction. A completely legal option permitting him to buy the stock in Roussel Rights, Inc., held by William Holt-Rymers crackled in his pocket. That ought to take care of Mr. Walter McCormack, who had no time to see busy policemen charged with, among other things, the responsibility for protecting him and his property. And without his property, Tibbs guessed, the austere Mr. McCormack might find the world a tough place to live in.

Traffic was crowded and slow on Wilshire Boulevard, particularly after Tibbs passed the Beverly Hilton headed east. He entered the colony of new high-rise buildings and searched for a parking lot without a full sign. With his license number he could have made use of a red-curb zone, but he was a firm believer in the principle that police powers carried with them police obligations. Two blocks past his destination he found a lot open, parked, and walked back.

Peterson was in and expecting him when he arrived. In contrast to the artist he had left a short time ago, Tibbs sensed an immediate hostility—in the office girl, who raised her too-plucked eyebrows before she announced him, and in the

118 *

broker when Virgil met him. He felt that he was in the camp of the enemy.

Peterson weighed about two hundred plus, with much of the plus concentrated around his middle. His frame was big and rugged, typical of the ex-football star, but he had obviously been neglecting himself and his stomach protruded. The athletic look was preserved in his crew cut, but denied by the network of tiny red veins that traced a discernible pattern across his broad, florid face. He held out a hamlike hand and shook hands as briefly as possible with no show of cordiality. He waved toward a chair as though he did not care whether Tibbs took it or not.

Peterson then seated himself behind his desk in a massive posture chair that would have held Nero Wolfe and spoke with a rasp in his voice uncommon in a salesman. "Please be brief," he directed. "I have an appointment."

Tibbs looked at him coolly as he sat down. "You have one with me," he reminded him. "This morning a man named Albert Roussel was buried in San Bernardino. He had been murdered. If you can tell me right now who killed him, and supply me with enough evidence to secure a conviction, I'll be glad to leave your office. Otherwise we have some things to talk over."

"I have nothing to tell you," Peterson snapped. "I knew the man and had business dealings with him. You know all this or you wouldn't have called me. But I have no evidence to give you. I hadn't seen Roussel for a long time—didn't even know he was in the country."

Tibbs took out his notebook. "You said you hadn't seen Dr. Roussel for a long time. How long would you estimate that to be?"

Peterson rocked back and forth, as though he were making a mighty effort to control himself. "Is that germane?" he asked. "I can't really see that it's any of your business."

Instead of flashing anger, Tibbs settled back and seemed to compose himself even more. When he spoke, his voice was smooth and controlled. "Mr. Peterson, a statement like that addressed to a police officer investigating a murder is asinine, and you know it. If you are trying to put yourself under suspicion, you are succeeding."

Peterson leaned forward and rose slightly to emphasize his bulk. "Are you here to pass judgment on me?" he barked.

Virgil maintained his calm. "I'm here to find out who killed Albert Roussel, and why. If, in the course of this conversation, you convince me that you are the person responsible, then I will arrest you and you will stand trial for your life."

The broker wiped his thick hand across his wide face. "I saw Roussel in Europe about three months ago. I was over there on other business and ran into him. We talked a little, but not to any great degree. Does that answer your question?"

"At that time did you discuss the Roussel Rights company?"

"Casually, very casually."

"Speaking of the company, how do you feel about the pending offer to purchase its assets?"

The broker leaned back and assumed the proper position for giving advice; his voice became more relaxed and impressive. "We have a very good offer and I am recommending that we take it. Particularly now with our inventive genius gone. Sooner or later some bright young man in a lab somewhere will come up with something new, and what we have now will be obsolete overnight. In the investment field, hanging on to something too long can be a bad mistake. Take a good profit when you can get it and then go for something else."

"That sounds logical," Virgil acknowledged. "Did Dr. Roussel agree with your advice? I say 'advice' since you are a professional in the field."

The touch of flattery had a clear effect. "Frankly we didn't discuss that. I'm not sure that the offer had been made at that time. It was largely a social call."

Tibbs' next question came as a surprise, as he intended it to. "Mr. Peterson, how long have you employed your present secretary?"

The muscles in the broker's big body went tight and he gripped the arms of his chair. "May I ask the reason for that question?" he asked, fighting to keep his voice under control.

Tibbs parried the question with an inconclusive answer. "I had the impression she was new," he replied with a degree of truth. "If she had been here for some time, I might have wanted to talk to her, too."

A shadow of relief crossed Peterson's face and the muscles of his shoulders relaxed. "You're quite right. She is new— joined me a little more than two months ago. But she has nothing whatever to do with my personal business arrangements."

Tibbs nodded that the answer was satisfactory and stood up. "Thank you for your time," he said, and left so promptly that Peterson was not required to stand up and shake hands once more.

On the way back to his office Virgil fought the traffic automatically while he turned the day's happenings over in his mind, sorting out the information he had been given from the lies he had been told. As he slowed down for the abrupt curves of the Pasadena Freeway, he gave most careful attention to three important facts that people had told him without intending to do so. For the first time he began to see a pattern emerging, but there were still too many gaps to permit him to draw even a tentative conclusion without more data.

For the next two days he would be unable to do anything further on the problem; he was scheduled to appear in court on a robbery case that would probably drag out while the due processes of law were employed to protect a man whose guilt was certain. Instead of bearding the hostile Walter McCormack, he would have to concentrate his attention on countering an attorney whose entire purpose would be to trap him in a single mistake.

Bob Nakamura was in when Virgil arrived, which was a break. "I need a hand again," Tibbs informed him. "It would help a lot."

Bob reached for a block of paper and a pencil. "Go ahead."

"In Beverly Hills there is a stockbroker I'm interested in— Oswald Peterson."

"The football star?"

"He was. I want a rundown on him—his financial standing and his personal life. If he has a family, I'd like an idea on how stable it is. Check also, if you can, on why he changed secretaries after he came back from Europe about ten weeks ago. I don't believe you can pin down what took him off to Europe, but get what you can."

"What sort of a guy is he?" Bob asked.

"Well, for one thing he's a bad liar," Virgil answered. "Possibly from lack of practice. He took me for an imbecile and I'm afraid I resented it."

"Don't blame you. I'll see what I can get. You're in court tomorrow, aren't you?"

Virgil nodded. "At least tomorrow, possibly longer."

Normally Tibbs did not mind giving evidence; it was part of his job and he was an experienced professional. This time he did mind, because he knew what the angle of attack would be. The accused was guilty and his lawyer would know it—as he would need to. Consequently he had asked for a jury trial, which was his legal right. With twelve citizens sitting in the box, most of whom had probably come from some other part of the country, there might be one or two who could be persuaded that the chief prosecution witness was not reliable because he was a Negro. Most defense attorneys would not attack in this manner; this particular one had no such reservations.

Before calling it a day, Virgil typed out a short note on plain paper to Walter McCormack, informing him that a stock option had been granted by William Holt-Rymers and that he would call concerning the matter. He signed it, dropped it into the outgoing mail, and then went home to prepare himself for the next day's ordeal.

It was a rough one. After the usual delays and motions, he gave his evidence clearly and concisely, aware that the whole case hung on his eyewitness report. When the defense attorney arose, he had a patronizing smile on his lips and the tough part began.

Since he had qualified as a police officer, it was a proper subject for cross-examination.

"Mr. Tibbs, how did you happen to be, ah—selected—as a member of the police department?" . . .

"Have you always lived in California, Mr. Tibbs?" . . .

"I'm interested in your boyhood in the Deep South, Officer Tibbs. I imagine it had a lot to do with forming the opinions you now hold."

"Objection!"

"Sustained."

"I withdraw the question. Officer Tibbs, have you revisited the area commonly known as the Deep South recently?"

"Yes, sir. I conducted a successful murder investigation down there a few weeks ago."

On it went, endless probing to find a weak spot—to make the jury wonder if racial considerations could be entirely ruled out of the evidence it had heard. Most police officers would not have to undergo this. Tibbs knew that it would be a long time before he would be free of this kind of harassment.

William Holt-Rymers was in a much more comfortable position. He sat in the big glassed-in kitchen at Sun Valley Lodge, far from the enforced formalities of the courtroom, talking with the Nunns, drinking coffee, and studying the light that streamed in through the windows. He was completely at ease. The nudity of the people around him did not disconcert him in the least. He was much more interested in the fact that they shared a common opinion of Virgil Tibbs as a police officer and as a man.

"I've always wanted to visit a nudist park," he said, opening a new topic. "A tight atmosphere kills good pictures; here you have all the ingredients necessary for freer, much better work. Gauguin proved that, although under somewhat different circumstances."

"Such as in his *Tahitian Mountain*," Forrest suggested.

Bill Rymers cocked an eyebrow and nodded approvingly. "And a dozen others. Some of his models were gifts from heaven and he made the most of them."

He finished his coffee and accepted a refill. "Frankly, I consider myself nearly as fortunate right here. I've spent ten minutes and already I've found a model worthy of any artist's attention."

Linda flushed with pleasure at the compliment. She had been photographed many times by excellent professional photographers, but had never seen herself through the medium of an artist's colors and interpretation.

"Would it upset your arrangements if I borrowed her for an hour or so?" Rymers asked his host.

Forrest glanced at Linda, who nodded a quick assent.

"Certainly not, Bill. That's what you're here for. And we know your reputation."

"Virgil briefed us," George admitted candidly.

"I may make a pest of myself," Rymers warned. "I may want to do several."

"We'd be honored," Emily said for the family. "How about a roll?"

"No, thank you. Later, if I may. I want to get started."

"May I watch?" Carole asked.

"If you promise to keep absolutely still and sit somewhere out of the way."

"I promise."

"Good. Then as soon as you're ready, Mrs. Nunn, we'll find the right place and begin."

"Me?" Emily asked with doubt in her voice.

"You," Rymers said firmly.

There was no respite for Tibbs the following day; the trial went on. Meanwhile George Nunn, after waiting somewhat impatiently for what he hoped was a decent interval, called Ellen Boardman and asked her for a date. Hesitatingly she had accepted—hesitating perhaps because of her recent grief, or their short acquaintance, or—quite possibly—because he helped to manage a nudist resort.

Determined to make a good impression, he chose a dark-brown sports coat, a pair of lighter slacks, and a lemon-colored tie suitable to the season. Upon his arrival he was presented to Ellen's parents, who were pleasant people, and for an hour he sat with them. At their request he once more detailed the discovery of the body and his futile attempt to breathe life back into it, remembering as he spoke that he was describing the death of the mother's brother. When it was over for what he hoped would be the last time, he had found a certain quiet understanding with these people who were trying to recover the normal pattern of their lives. He liked them and hoped earnestly that they liked him as well.

Finally he excused himself and, with Ellen beside him, drove with extra care down the mountain road toward San Bernardino. He and his date played miniature golf, had dinner, and saw a movie. When the evening was over, he regretfully turned his car back toward the Big Bear Lake area and the long climb up the mountain. Tonight he did not mind the distance or the time it would take; he felt a sense of mild excitement when Ellen leaned back and let the air play with her hair. She had her eyes shut and George slowed the car down slightly in order to suit her mood.

"What are you going to do?" she asked suddenly.

"Do? With my life, is that what you mean?"

"Yes."

George guided the car around a curve and bit into the first grade. "I'm planning to be a marine architect; I studied it in college. I love the sea and I love boats. Because they go places, I guess, instead of just standing still. Even if it's only out to Catalina and back every weekend, it's still movement—something dynamic that isn't cut and dried."

Ellen opened her eyes and looked at him. "When I was a little girl, I used to daydream about taking a fine oceangoing yacht and sailing out over the Pacific to see the world."

"That's a wonderful dream," George said. "Don't lose it. A lot of people feel the same way. The only thing that stops them is the cost—it takes time and money. But then so does everything else."

"I've never had any money and I don't particularly want any," Ellen answered. "Some of the moneyed people who come to our place aren't very nice. We have our problems now and then."

"So do we. The usual ones and a few more, because ours is a nudist resort. A few people still think it's some kind of an open-air—" He stopped in embarrassment.

"I understand," Ellen said. She fell silent briefly and George wondered if he had offended her. Then she asked, "George, how did you and your family become involved in—the kind of business you operate?"

"Personal conviction—I think that's the best answer. I know you probably don't see it the way we do, but there are things to consider. You might remember the bathing suits of a couple of generations ago. Now gradually we're coming to the point of admitting ourselves to be human, and without somehow being ashamed of it."

"Still, to go without *any* clothes at all . . ."

George let the matter hang there; he was too content with her company just as she was. He guided the car over a rise and the waxing three-quarter moon flooded them with its cool, impersonal light.

Ellen nodded toward a turnoff ahead. "Stop there, will you?" she requested.

George swung the car off the road and onto the gravel of one of the many viewpoint parking lots. He stopped and set the brake.

"I've always loved this particular place," Ellen said simply.

George came around and helped her out of the car. As they walked toward the stone balustrade that guarded the edge, he was close enough to touch her; he didn't, because he sensed it would not be welcome—at least not yet.

From the ledge on the mountain the view spread out below them was spectacular. Though the moonlight was swallowed up in the atmosphere and showed nothing of the land below, the lights of the city and of Norton Air Force Base spread a jeweled carpet at the feet of the night.

Ellen sat on the low stone wall and turned her head to look down at the spectacle. As she did so, George studied her faint profile and the way she held herself even in repose; new ideas began to stir in his mind about her even though this was only the second time they had met. He lifted his wrist and tilted it so that he could see the hands on the dial.

Ellen noticed him and asked quickly, "What time is it?"

"Five minutes after twelve."

She rose to her feet. "Another day."

"Yes, a new day." He decided to share a small personal thing. "My birthday," he added.

"Many happy returns," she said as they walked back to the car.

"I hope so—and I hope in the same company." He paused, aware he had betrayed his thoughts. "What I mean is, this seems like the best possible way to start the day."

She looked at him. "How nice of you," she said with a smile. As he returned it, she stopped suddenly and turned halfway toward him.

"Happy birthday," she said. She lifted her head and parted her lips slightly.

It was one of the few impulsive things she had ever done. She was not in the habit of allowing herself to be kissed except by very old friends, and then only infrequently.

To George she was at that moment utterly desirable. The touch of her warm lips electrified him; he had to restrain himself from crushing her hard against him.

A car came up the hill and swept the parking area with its lights as it made the curve. George continued to hold her during the moment they were on display and after the car had passed. Then he gently released her and found himself unsure on his feet as he guided her back across the gravel.

When he dropped her off at her parents' lodge, he did not attempt to kiss her again. He wished her good night and drove back to Sun Valley contented with himself and the world. The next step would be to find out if she could sail a boat; if not, he could teach her.

chapter 12

When Virgil Tibbs arrived a few minutes before eight to keep his evening appointment with Walter McCormack, he found Walter Brown waiting for him at the entrance to the estate. As soon as Virgil pulled his car up before the iron grillwork, the chauffeur recognized him and swung open the gates that guarded the private drive. Tibbs paused to thank him.

"I got orders to let you in," Brown told him. "How'd you manage to get invited?"

"It took some work," Virgil admitted. "He did invite me, though, so no one is going to get fired."

"I know that, but how you got the old goat to give in I can't figure. Park right up by the door—nobody else is coming."

As Virgil guided his car up the curving driveway, daylight was still strong on the glittering water and the wind from the west was charged with the salty tang of the ocean. He paused for a moment after he got out of his car to look out over the long coastline and fill his lungs with the fresh, inviting air. Then, regretfully directing his mind back to business, he pushed the bell and waited to be admitted.

Walter McCormack received him in his study; he was seated behind what could only be a wealthy man's desk and seemed in no haste to rise. He was thin and of slight build, probably in his early seventies. He wore a cashmere coat that was severely cut in a conservative pattern; its narrow lapels emphasized his thin long nose, which divided his face like a hatchet blade. For a quick moment Virgil thought of Lombroso, the Italian criminologist who maintained that a person's character was revealed in the set of his features. Although that theory had long since ben disproved, Walter McCormack did look the aristocrat, fully accustomed to imposing his will on others. As Tibbs entered the room, McCormack at last rose halfway to his feet and offered a thin hand, which was cool to the touch. "Sit down, Mr. Tibbs," he said formally.

He waited until his guest was comfortable and then continued as though in the same breath.

"Suppose we come right to the point and save each other a great deal of time. We are both fully aware that the stock option you hold is a device and nothing more. You are a police officer of good repute, but with no outside financial resources. You could not possibly afford to exercise the option that you hold, and it is therefore worthless."

"Quite," Virgil agreed without turning a hair.

"Very well. Let me add that when you first called my home had I been told that a police officer wished to see me officially, you would not have needed to resort to ridiculous extremes to arrange an appointment. For this I apologize; my instructions to my staff did not anticipate such a contingency."

"I'm very relieved to hear that," Tibbs answered. He folded his hands in his lap. "It's very seldom that a responsible citizen refuses to see a policeman."

"Obviously. Now, what can I do for you?"

Virgil opened his notebook; with this man he did not fear the psychological results of doing so. "As you will have surmised, I am investigating the death of Dr. Albert Roussel."

"Are you the officer in charge?"

"For the present at least, I am."

"All right, what are your questions?"

Virgil got down to business. "How well did you know the deceased?"

"Very well—over a period of several years."

"To your knowledge did he have any enemies in this country who might have been waiting for his return?"

"Unequivocally no. I seriously doubt that he ever had an enemy in the world. Dr. Roussel had a rare gift for making himself liked everywhere he went. Also there was nothing in his work to generate hatred."

Tibbs took a moment to look at a magnificent sea painting that hung over the fireplace. "Is there a possibility he might have anticipated someone else's patents or research—innocently, of course?"

McCormack shook his head and settled down further behind his desk. "Extremely doubtful. If any parallel work was being done, I am quite sure I would know of it. Dr. Roussel was a highly original research worker who plowed new ground wherever he turned his mind and interests."

Virgil made a note, writing for several seconds before he resumed the conversation. "May I ask your opinion, sir, regarding the offer to buy out Roussel Rights?"

McCormack gave him a shrewd look. "You aren't thinking of trying to sell your option, are you?"

Tibbs shook his head, letting it go at that.

McCormack continued, "The offer was originally made

with the assumption that Dr. Roussel would continue actively in his research into photographic chemistry. That is of course impossible now. Despite this misfortune, the patents we hold are basic and have a considerable time to run. Each year the royalties paid have increased, and there is no sign of a letdown. Is that sufficient information?"

"I believe so. Since you are the business manager for the company, I presume you can tell me what is now likely to happen to Dr. Roussel's personal beholdings."

McCormack thought that over as he rubbed the end of his nose. "I see no harm in telling you," he said at last. "The information will be public in a few days, and of course I realize the importance of the job you are doing."

He shifted and sat up a little straighter in his chair. He remained a small man, but one with an aura of dignity that gave him a measure of strength.

"Dr. Roussel had only one living close relative—his sister Margaret, toward whom he felt very close. However, for very sound reasons she is not his heir."

Virgil lifted an eyebrow and waited for more.

"Margaret is married and has a daughter, a suitable and proper young woman. I don't know if you are aware of this, Mr. Tibbs—you probably are—but where major sums of money are concerned, it is quite usual to skip one generation in making a bequest. If I were fortunate enough to have descendants, I would leave my estate to my grandson. It would be understood within the family that my son would use and administer the funds as long as he lived and remained capable. Upon his death my grandson would then take over without the necessity of paying another inheritance tax. Dr. Roussel observed that principle in leaving his estate to his niece. Actually Margaret is a member of his own generation, so the legacy is going down only one step instead of two."

For a moment Virgil Tibbs remained silent. "Will Miss Boardman have any say concerning her legacy? I put that badly; I meant to ask if her mother will assume full control or if she herself will be consulted."

This time McCormack did some thinking before he replied. "Knowing the family as I do, I would assume that Ellen will be regarded as the heir and her parents will advise her only if they are consulted. Mr. Boardman is a retiring person who is doing exactly what he wants to do, and the same largely pertains to his wife. They have all the money they want for themselves. They are genuinely happy people who have no desire for world travel or anything like that."

"People to be envied," Tibbs said.

"Agreed."

A maid entered the room with a small box and a glass of water. McCormack took them, swallowed a pill, and handed them back. "What is your choice of refreshment?" he asked.

"Anything cold, if it isn't too much trouble," Virgil answered. He knew better than to refuse.

When the girl had left, Tibbs picked up the conversation. "Mr. McCormack, what I have to discuss with you now is confidential."

"Very well." The financier nodded.

"You are aware, of course, that there is apparently an even division of opinion among the surviving stockholders concerning the sale of the company."

"Yes. Mrs. Pratt and Mr. Peterson want to sell; Mr. Holt-Rymers and I are opposed to the idea."

"Do you know how Dr. Roussel would have voted?"

"I do. He would have opposed the sale."

"Is this your opinion, sir, or are you stating a known fact?"

"I am stating a known fact. Dr. Roussel wrote to me privately on the matter. I can produce the letter, if you wish."

Virgil Tibbs felt a great sense of relief; one important fact had been pinned down. He kept his face composed with an effort when he spoke. "For the present, at least, your statement is quite sufficient. Now, another matter. When I called on her, Mrs. Pratt told me that she and Dr. Roussel were to have been married shortly after the stockholders' meeting. Might that have changed Dr. Roussel's view of the matter?"

McCormack sat suddenly erect. "I don't believe it," he said emphatically. "I'm not questioning your statement, but I can't accept Joyce's that she and Albert were to have been married. At one time, many years ago, Albert was quite fond of her—a sort of collegiate puppy-love affair. Later on he completely outgrew that sentiment and she remained, at the most, a friend. She helped organize and finance the company because she knew a good thing, but it was strictly a business matter."

"You would say, then, that Mrs. Pratt was lying to me?" Tibbs asked.

McCormack answered without flinching, "I can't interpret it any other way. If Albert had any such ideas, he would have let me know since it concerned the company. I might say," he added, "that Dr. Roussel and I were a lot closer than many people knew, Mrs. Pratt included."

The maid re-entered with a tray, which she set beside Tibbs. On it were two Pilsner-type glasses and two plain ones filled with ice, a choice of two imported brands of beer, and an assortment of four bottled soft drinks. When Virgil indicated a lemon-lime mix, she uncapped it and poured it into an iced glass. In deference to his guest McCormack made a similar choice and then waited until they were once more alone.

"Mr. Peterson?" Tibbs asked, knowing he would be understood.

"A brash and careless opportunist. He had an early success based entirely on his football fame; then the going got rougher. He advised several clients badly and they lost money. He came with us after meeting Joyce Pratt at a party and falling a little under her spell. That is, assuming she has one, which is open to question."

"In my case, definitely," Tibbs agreed. "Is Mr. Peterson married?"

"Yes, but I believe he is now involved in divorce proceedings."

"Recently instituted?" Tibbs asked with interest.

"Yes, although the trouble dates back a few years, I understand."

"Do you consider Mr. Peterson to be truthful and reliable in his statements?"

"I'm afraid I think he would say whatever he felt would do him the most good."

"Do you know why he went to Europe about three months ago?"

"He said business, but I know of no business he has that would involve him in such a trip."

"At the risk of appearing irrelevant, where do you customarily hold your board meetings, or other business conferences?"

"Here. Possibly out of respect for my senior status. I send

my car for Mrs. Pratt. The others come by themselves."

Tibbs sipped at his drink. His throat was dry from talking. "You have been most helpful," he said when he was finished. "Have you any idea who killed Dr. Roussel?"

McCormack leaned back in his chair and thought for a full half minute. "No," he said finally. "I have a suspicion, but it is an unfair one and I have no evidence whatsoever to support it."

Virgil took a final drink from his glass and rose to his feet. "If it becomes necessary or desirable, Mr. McCormack, for me to see you again, may I phone you?"

McCormack looked at him evenly. "Of course you can. I am assuming, Mr. Tibbs, that like everyone else you regard my seclusion as arbitrary. Allow me to assure you that it is not." He stopped and tasted his own drink.

"I keep very much to myself because it has been forced on me. My wife is dead. We had no children. I have no living relatives, as far as I know. I do have a substantial financial holding and this is the source of my difficulty."

He paused, but Tibbs did not interrupt.

"You would never believe the extent to which I have been plagued by requests and demands for money. Some were worthy, of course, but others were totally selfish. The fact that I am getting old and have no heirs has focused attention on me. People have pushed their way into my home and have even invaded my bedroom at night. I have been subjected to every artifice and subterfuge imaginable; I could write a definitive treatise on human greed. It is unlimited, Mr. Tibbs, and it is sometimes absolutely conscienceless. It will betray anyone and will even resort to murder, as I fear you know all too well. My only defense has been to shut myself away from everyone and forgo the normal pleasures that lie outside my gate. I am well taken care of here and I have provided generously for my staff, although I have not told them so."

Virgil listened, taking in the full meaning of McCormack's words. When the older man had finished, Tibbs said, "Thank you for your help. As far as I am able, I'll respect your privacy. Understanding your reasons, let me say that I don't think I would care to trade with you. Even if I could—in all respects."

McCormack understood. "Your day is coming," he said. "The restrictions that have been imposed on your people are vanishing, as they must. And you wouldn't wish to trade your years for mine."

McCormack rose and for the first time came out from behind his desk. He walked toward Tibbs with a curious stiffness; Virgil glanced at his feet and saw the unbroken smoothness of the shoes that had never been flexed. "Please don't—" he began.

McCormack waved him to silence. "I lost my legs more than fifty years ago and I have done very nicely without them ever since." He came over and shook hands. "A railroad train cut them off. I invested the settlement I received and was very fortunate. At such a price I bought my independence."

Virgil drove home with a curious mixture of emotions. He realized that though he had been warned to expect a ruthless aristocrat, he liked Walter McCormack and for that reason, as well as others, hoped that the financier had been telling him the truth.

chapter 13

Shortly after nine the following morning, which was Saturday, Walter McCormack personally made a long-distance telephone call. A few minutes thereafter his comfortable, air-conditioned black Cadillac purred down his private drive, swung through the gateway, and turned eastward. Almost two hours later it pulled up smoothly under Brown's expert guidance in the driveway of Pine Shadows Lodge. The chauffeur held the rear door open while the owner emerged. Then, for more than an hour and a half, the financier conferred with Ellen Boardman and her parents.

When the meeting was over, Ellen left McCormack talking with her parents and, pushing open the front door of the lodge, stepped out into the shade of the tall trees. She shook her head and automatically brushed the sides of her hair back into place. She seemed to be almost unaware of her surroundings. She was realizing that being rich didn't fit into her own picture of her life at all.

It had been impressed upon her that the responsibility had been given to her and she must assume it: there was no doubt that she would have to deal with it. Walter McCormack had offered to guide and assist her, but she still felt quite unprepared for the role of heiress.

In the driveway, almost like a symbol of her new status,

was the impressive black sedan and, seated behind the wheel, the waiting chauffeur. She looked at the man and the machine, trying to clear her mind and assemble her thoughts.

Then she became aware that the man who was patiently sitting in the car was a Negro: that brought a quick image of Virgil Tibbs, the remarkable man whose abilities she had begun to appreciate. She advanced a step or two nearer the car and, when the chauffeur looked up at her, wished him good morning.

"Good morning, Ma'am," Brown answered.

She noted an accent that Virgil Tibbs did not have; the "g" was all but lost.

"Would you like to come inside?" she asked. "I can find you something cool to drink if you're thirsty."

"No thank you, Ma'am," Brown answered. "I'm all right, thanks just the same." He gave her a faint smile as he spoke, but there was restraint in it. He was not, she decided regretfully, another Virgil Tibbs.

Then, as though aware that the initiative had all been hers, Brown made an effort to be agreeable. "Real nice place you got here," he offered.

"Yes, we like it," Ellen answered. "And our guests seem to, too."

"I can sure see why," Brown commented. "I always like to see trees and things like that."

So did Ellen. "You'll pass the best view when you go back down the mountain," she said. "You have to turn off at the bottom of the first hill. There's a parking area there. The view is spectacular. I usually stop to see it."

"I'd like to do that, Ma'am," Brown responded. "But you

better tell Mr. McCormack about it. If he wants to stop, then we stop. If he don't wanna, then we don't."

The reply chilled Ellen and made her regret having opened the conversation. She'd meant to be kind, but had only succeeded in underlining the chauffeur's subservient position. Before she could think further about it, the door opened behind her and Walter McCormack appeared.

He nodded to Brown and said, "We'll be going now," and then he turned to her. "I think we've pretty well discussed it all now, and I know how you must feel," he said. "I've been through it myself, under different circumstances. Don't worry about it. Just remember the things I told you. And if anything comes up you're not certain about, give me a call. You have my number."

With Brown holding the door, he climbed unassisted into the back of his car and settled down onto the cushions. The dust raised by the tires was still in the air when the phone rang in the lodge. Ellen answered it and heard George Nunn's voice on the line.

"I'd like very much to see you this evening," he said. "Will you be free?"

Informed as she had just been, Ellen thought momentarily that his interest in her might well be because of her sudden transformation into an heiress. Then she realized he would have no way of knowing, and he certainly did not impress her as the fortune-hunting kind.

"What did you have in mind?" she asked.

"We're having a dance here at the lodge tonight. I'd like very much to have you come. Just informal dress," he added quickly.

Ellen hesitated and then decided to go. She wanted to see George again and in his own element; since everyone would be dressed, it would be a good opportunity. Although she had been at the nudist resort once briefly, she still had a considerable curiosity concerning the place. She accepted and they agreed on the time.

Then, while planning what to wear to the dance, she found herself wondering if Virgil Tibbs was making any progress in the investigation of her uncle's murder. There was still the unsettling possibility that George or a member of his family might be involved—if not in the actual murder, through some knowledge of it that was being kept to themselves. She glanced at the calendar to make sure it was Saturday. She assumed that the work of finding out who had done the horrible thing would have been halted for the weekend.

In that she was wrong, for Virgil Tibbs had already been in his office for more than two hours, sorting out the notes he had taken and fitting together the bits and pieces he had managed to obtain. A newspaper lay on his desk; on the front page it reported the conviction of the man he had testified against earlier in the week. That closed the matter unless they released him on parole too soon, and then the whole weary job would have to be done all over again. Crime was the only way of life, the only trade, the convicted man knew.

The mail came in and Virgil glanced at the pile. A blue-and-white envelope with the return address of Sun Valley Lodge caught his eye. Before he opened it, he glanced over to see if a similar one might by any chance be on Bob Nakamura's desk. It was there.

He slit the envelope open and drew out the combination brochure and membership-application form. There were attractive pictures of the pool, tennis court, volleyball courts, and other facilities. One paragraph of the printed text had been crossed out in ink and a handwritten note had been added in the margin. The deleted paragraph read:

Singles. Under no circumstances will married singles be accepted for membership, a married single being defined as an adult who applies without his or her spouse. Single adult men and women will be issued memberships only on a quota basis in order to maintain the family atmosphere of the park. The decision in each case will depend on the individual applicant and the action of the membership committee will be final.

Next to this, in a slanting feminine hand, was written:

Having VIP status, your welcome is assured. Please come.

LINDA

Although he had not the slightest intention of accepting, Virgil was very pleased that he had been asked. His spirits lifted and the monotonous work he had been doing suddenly seemed more interesting. He was still turning the heart-warming thought over in his mind when Bob Nakamura came in accompanied by a very attractive brunette and two small children.

Tibbs got to his feet. "Hello, Amiko," he said. "Welcome to the treadmill. By the way, Bob, your membership application for the nudist park just arrived. It's in your mail."

"Nudist park? You didn't tell me about that," Amiko gasped.

Bob tore open the envelope and glanced at the folder it contained. Then he calmly handed it to his wife.

The two men waited while she looked at it, examined the

pictures, and even read the application blank on the back. "I don't think we can afford it," she said finally. "Although it might be a good thing for the children."

Tibbs glanced at his watch. "Why don't we all have some lunch?" he suggested. As he spoke, the phone rang.

He picked it up and listened for almost two minutes. As soon as he hung up, he pressed his lips together, looked again at his watch, and made a careful note. He left it significantly on his desk and glanced at Bob, who barely nodded. This done, Virgil scooped up the younger of the Nakamura children and said, "Let's go and eat, shall we?"

While Virgil was shepherding Amiko and her youngsters out into the corridor, Bob crossed the room and read the note:

12:46 P.M. Walter McCormack phoned to say he had called on Ellen Boardman this morning to advise her of her inheritance. He talked to her for some time. She now holds the balance of power regarding the sale of the company. McC. advised her against selling, but when the news gets out, he expects she will be subject to some pressures.

Below the message Virgil had drawn three horizontal lines in red.

A little after four that afternoon Joyce Pratt called Ellen long distance. "My dear, I've wanted to talk to you before this," she said, "but in view of the circumstances I felt you would like to be by yourself for a little while."

"That was very thoughtful of you," Ellen replied.

"As you know, your uncle and I were very close and dear friends for many years; he spoke of you so much that I feel

I know you very well. I think now we should meet and have a chance to really get to know each other."

"I'd be happy to do that," Ellen said. Her comment was more courtesy than truth. She also was aware that Mrs. Pratt had organized the Roussel holding company and was a stockholder, a circumstance that made a meeting almost a necessity.

"Do come and have dinner with me tomorrow," Joyce invited. "I have tickets for the Hollywood Bowl. Do you like music?"

Ellen considered quickly. Her parents were back with the car, so she could go if she really wanted to. And, she thought, since she would have to face up to her new responsibilities soon, she might as well begin now. Determined that she would not allow herself to be panicked into anything, she accepted the invitation. If everything went well, fine; if it did not, she could call either Walter McCormack, whom she already trusted, or possibly Virgil Tibbs.

Then she remembered that Tibbs was a policeman, pure and simple, and she could hardly call upon him to help her solve her personal problems—and her financial problems *were* personal.

At that moment the phone rang again. She brushed her hair aside and put the instrument against her ear. "Pine Shadows Lodge," she said.

"This is Virgil Tibbs, Miss Boardman, how are you?"

"Very well, thank you."

Now, was *he* going to invite her somewhere?

"I called to tell you that Mr. McCormack has informed me of his visit with you this morning, and the purpose behind it."

"Yes."

"I want to ask for your close cooperation, because it is very important. Let me stress that—*very* important."

"I understand," she said.

"Good. Will you please call me immediately, collect, if anything whatever happens concerning your new status. For instance, I want to know if anyone else comes to see you—if *anyone* calls you—who might have any possible connection with the matter we are both interested in. I don't care if you call me a dozen times a day, I want to know at once anything and everything that happens. Is that perfectly clear?"

"Yes, it is. I can give you a report right now, if you would like."

"Please."

"George Nunn called me this morning and invited me to a dance at his parents' lodge this evening. I accepted." A sudden thought came to her. "It will be dressed, of course," she added hastily.

"Naturally. I see no reason why you shouldn't go. Is that all?"

"No. Mrs. Joyce Pratt called me. Do you know her?"

"Yes, I do. Go ahead."

"She phoned just a little while ago. She said that in view of the circumstances we ought to meet. She asked me for dinner tomorrow and said she had tickets for the Hollywood Bowl."

"Are you going?"

"Yes, I am." She hesitated, and made up her mind. "May I ask you something?"

"What would you like to know?"

"Maybe I shouldn't ask you this, and if that's the case I'm

sorry, but is there any progress in—the matter that concerns us both?"

There was silence for a few moments on the line; then the answer came. "Yes, Miss Boardman, there is. If I trust you, will you respect my confidence?"

"Most certainly."

"Very well, then. Not to be repeated to *anyone*, I will tell you this much: I am confident I know what happened, why, and who was responsible."

"You know *who*?" Ellen asked, her voice tight.

"Yes, I know. But knowing and proving are two entirely different things. I am still gathering proof. If you say one word of this to anyone, you might make the job infinitely harder."

"You can trust me," Ellen said. "Is the danger all past?"

There was another slight pause. "No, Miss Boardman, I wouldn't say that it is. That is why I want you to keep me continually informed of your movements."

For the next few hours Ellen Boardman lived in a thick haze. The hand of murder, which had struck her uncle, now seemed to be groping toward her. She saw again the cold still face lying on the slab in San Bernardino and she had a sudden urge to flee somewhere and hide. She was not a coward, but all her life she had avoided trouble simply by not inviting it. Now trouble was being forced upon her and she felt inadequate and defenseless. She thought of canceling her engagement for the evening, then remembered that Virgil Tibbs had told her he saw no reason why she shouldn't go.

How far, she wondered, could she trust his assurances? But

then she recalled how he had anticipated her thoughts about visiting George's parents, and she felt a little easier. She would have to trust him. If he was not competent, then his superiors would never have assigned him to handle the case.

When George came to pick her up, she was ready. As they drove down the mountain in the dying light of what had been another lovely day, she still could not relax the unrelenting parade of her thoughts. But out of the bewilderment that surrounded her, one clear and welcome idea emerged: it couldn't have been George or Virgil Tibbs would never have approved their being together now. She did not want it to be George. Despite his odd background, she knew that she liked him and was enjoying his company.

Sun Valley Lodge, when they arrived, seemed just like any other resort where a dance was taking place. In what George described as the clubhouse she found a sizable crowd, a six-piece orchestra, and a pattern of paper decorations overhead that helped to create a holiday atmosphere. When Linda came to greet them, smiling and thoroughly attractive in a powder-blue dance dress, Ellen determined to put everything else out of her mind and enjoy herself as she wanted to do.

In George's arms she danced and was happy. Each time the music stopped, there was someone new to be her next partner. She warmed to the atmosphere and to the friendly people; she was feeling totally rid of the problems that had plagued her when Linda appeared with a couple in tow.

"Ellen, this is Amiko and Bob," Linda introduced. In a few moments Ellen was dancing smoothly with the first Nisei who had ever taken her out onto a dance floor. She liked him immediately and smiled at him as they danced. "I'm glad to see you so relaxed and happy, Miss Boardman," he said, smiling back at her.

Every muscle in her body tightened; she had never met him before and had been introduced only as Ellen. Mechanically she kept her feet moving, but the rhythm was gone.

Her companion sensed the abrupt change and responded to it "I'm Bob Nakamura," he explained. "Pasadena police. I'm Virgil Tibbs' partner."

She relaxed a little, as much as she could. "Did he send you?" she asked.

Bob nodded. "The Nunn family knows all about it. As far as the rest are concerned, we're prospective members. And please don't let it alarm you, but we're going to keep a pretty close eye on you for the next few days. Until after the board meeting."

"But that's about two weeks away," Ellen reminded him.

"Perhaps not. Virgil is seeing McCormack this evening to try and get it moved up—to force someone's hand, if you follow me."

Ellen felt a strange and frightening feeling in the bottom of her stomach. "Am I to be a guinea pig?" she asked.

"No, we wouldn't do that to you—not if we could help it, at any rate. Virgil has something going and he wants to get a certain person off balance, as I told you."

"I understand," Ellen said.

"Good. Then go ahead and enjoy yourself. It's a nice party."

Instead of following his advice, Ellen put her head close to his shoulder so that she could speak softly over the music. "Can I trust George Nunn?" she asked.

Bob turned her effortlessly and took a few steps before he replied. "As far as I know you can. Virgil didn't say anything to the contrary."

Ellen frowned. If George was completely dependable, why would Virgil Tibbs have sent his partner to watch over her at the dance? His answer had sounded like an evasion; where she had wanted firm assurance, it had not been given.

She managed the rest of the evening well enough, but she was too deeply troubled now to recapture her former happy mood. As soon as she decently could, she asked to be taken home.

As the car began to wend its way up the mountain road toward the high plateau that housed Big Bear Lake, George broke what had become a long and awkward silence. "Ellen," he began, "forgive me for bringing this up, but has Virgil given you any indication about how things are going?"

Ellen tried not to let the increased tension she felt show; she was afraid of betraying herself. "I haven't seen him recently," she answered truthfully.

George negotiated a curve while he searched for the right words. "I don't know just how to put this," he said with some hesitation. "I don't want to talk about unpleasant things, but until a lot of questions are answered, I'm a little worried."

"I can understand that," she responded tersely.

"Here's what I'm getting at: I like you—you know that. And I've got a lot of confidence in Virgil—I've seen a little of what he can do. But until he comes up with the final answers, if you at any time would like to have—"

He stopped speaking and wheeled the car almost savagely around one of the viewpoint turnouts. "I'm sorry. Let's try again. Are all your guest rooms filled?"

"No."

"All right, then. Any time you're worried in any way, or think there's any danger, please call me. Night or day, it doesn't matter. I'm not the world's greatest, but I can handle myself reasonably well and"—he paused to think once more before he shaped the words—"and I'd like to—to help," he concluded.

Ellen turned her head and looked at him. "Do you mean that?" she asked.

"Yes," George answered, looking straight ahead. "I do. If I caught anyone trying to hurt you, I think I would kill him with my bare hands."

As soon as he had spoken, he wondered if he'd sounded too theatrical. He hadn't meant it to be that way.

Ellen did not answer with words. Instead she slid across the seat until she was next to him. He responded by putting his right arm across her shoulders for a moment, then withdrew it when he had to make another turn on the mountain road.

When they reached the lodge, he pulled up under the deep shade of the trees and set the parking brake. He was in no hurry to leave her, and obviously she was willing to let their evening together last a few more moments. They sat listening to the sounds of the night and watching the faint light of the waxing moon filter down through the few places where it could penetrate to the ground. Then, for a frightening instant, George was startled by the thought that something might be lurking, even at that moment, shielded by the blackness of the night, waiting to strike. He deliberately banished the thought. He had been theatrical just a few minutes before and he did not want to repeat the blunder, even in his mind.

He turned to Ellen and looked at her. She gazed back at him with a steadiness that, even in the night darkness, sent a welcome shiver down his backbone. He reached out his right arm, gathered her in gently, and kissed her once, long and tenderly. Then he opened the door, walked around the car, and helped her out. As he saw her to her door, he reflected that he'd meant it when he said he would kill with his bare hands, if need be, to protect her.

Inside her room Ellen shut her eyes for a moment as though to black out her thoughts; then she shook her head and slowly began to undress. George had kissed her and she knew she had wanted him to.

Quietly she slipped out of her clothes. For just a moment, before she put on her nightgown, she paused to look at herself in the mirror. Her figure was certainly not spectacular in any way, but it was presentable. That was an odd word, she thought—presentable. What was it like, she wondered, to be a nudist? She could not answer her own question as she slipped the gown over her head and climbed into bed.

Monday was an exceptionally busy day for Virgil Tibbs. He visited several banks and talked with senior officers concerning the accounts of certain people in whom he was interested. At one of them he was shown to a vacant booth next to the safe-deposit vault and, because of his standing as a police officer and the gravity of the matter he was investigating, he was allowed to go over a series of canceled checks that had not yet been mailed back to the client. One of these checks interested him very much; he arranged to have it photostated on both sides and took the print with him when he left.

The next stop was the county recorder's office in Los Angeles, where he looked up an item in the real-estate records. From the center he walked over to the *Times* building and arrived in time for an appointment he had made to talk with the art critic. This turned into a fairly extended conversation. From the *Times* building he phoned the Retail Credit Bureau and obtained some further information. With these three things accomplished, he reclaimed his car and took the freeway back to Pasadena, where Bob Nakamura was waiting for him. Bob had done his part and had a reasonably full report on the background and activities of Oswald Peterson, the broker.

In accordance with his usual habit, Virgil made individual notes on each piece of information he had learned and laid the slips out in a geometric pattern on top of his desk. With the other notes he already had, he began a process of shifting that looked like a new form of solitaire. In this manner he grouped related facts together and determined where there were blanks that needed to be filled.

Presently he noted a gap in the parade of data before him and picked up the telephone; in a few moments he had the records section of the Los Angeles Police Department on the line. He identified himself and then asked a question, waited while the necessary information was looked up, and received a negative answer. That suited him entirely; he made out another three-by-five card and fitted it neatly into place. When a teletype came up from the first floor about thumbprints on driving licenses, one more card was added to Virgil's careful accumulation.

The phone interrupted him. When he answered, it was the secretary of the Japanese-American Gardeners Association returning his earlier call. A short conversation clarified another point and allowed one of the few remaining gaps in the maze-like pattern on his desk to be filled.

At this point he picked up the phone once more, dialed the operator, and asked to speak with Miss Ellen Boardman at Pine Shadows Lodge. "How did your evening go with Mrs. Pratt?" he asked her when she came on the wire.

"Oh, quite well. Over dinner she made a considerable point about her business experience and pointed out all the evidence of her success."

"She did that to me, too," Virgil said.

"After that she carefully patronized me quite a lot. I was the sweet young thing not yet quite awake in the world. She offered to become my guide and mentor and explain everything to me."

"Did she mention your stockholding?" Tibbs asked.

"Oh, only indirectly. She knew about it, of course. She did ask me if I planned to attend the stockholders' meeting and said she would talk with me about it later. Of course that's almost two weeks away."

"Not any more it isn't," Tibbs said grimly. "Mr. McCormack has moved it up to this weekend."

"Oh? I remember hearing something about that. Why did he do it?"

"Because I asked him to. How was the concert?"

"Oh, it was very nice. I love the Bowl, although I don't get there very often. And we had coffee afterward."

"Yes, I know."

"You do? How?" Ellen asked.

"You had a police officer with you most of the evening. He enjoyed the concert, too."

"Goodness, did he follow me home? I thought there was a car behind me most of the way."

"He did part of the way, then someone else took over. Which reminds me, could you accommodate another couple for a few days beginning tomorrow?"

"Yes. Why? Are they—friends of yours?"

"In a way of speaking. Mr. and Mrs. Mooney will be arriving tomorrow morning for a week's stay. Mr. Mooney is the officer who stopped by a few days ago to ask if anyone who'd had a reservation had failed to appear."

"Oh—I remember."

"Good. Of course the fact that he is a police officer is something you don't discuss, but if anyone asks you about it, don't deny it. In that case let him know immediately."

"I will."

Ellen hung up slightly confused. Obviously she was being given a bodyguard, which was a new experience for her. In a way she welcomed it, but in a way it was distressing.

The following morning Dick and Elaine Mooney checked in at Pine Shadows and proved to be thoroughly agreeable. Ellen found that it was a considerable comfort to have the young officer there—a person she could definitely trust who would be on hand if he was needed. But she was still off balance when George Nunn called her and suggested a date on Wednesday; she hedged and asked him to call back again.

Later that afternoon Virgil Tibbs had a conference with Captain Lindholm and outlined his plan of action to the senior officer for approval. When that meeting was over, he returned to his apartment, showered, and ate a fairly light dinner, in view of what he had planned for the evening. An hour later, clad in a white training *gi* tied with the black belt that it had taken him so many years of hard work to earn, he began a two-hour training session in the karate *dojo* with the few present who were his equals and the two who were his betters.

When it was all over, he showered once more and stepped on the scales; the pointer stopped at a hundred and sixty-one pounds, six more than when he had first joined the force. At that time he had barely made the hundred-and-fifty-five-pound minimum. His abdomen was still hard and flat, and despite the fact that he was naturally slender in build, the muscles that rippled under his dark skin understood their functions and had been conditioned by constant training.

Virgil Tibbs dressed and returned to his apartment with a sense of well-being. He was relaxed as he turned on his stereo and stacked the changer with Ravel's *Introduction and Allegro*, Falla's *Nights in the Gardens of Spain*, and a performance recording of Duke Ellington at Newport. He mixed himself a drink and leaned back to listen. He needed the atmosphere that the music provided and the chance to let his thoughts wander away from the hard realities they would have to face in the morning.

The next day would be Wednesday, two days before the board meeting. More than that, it was to be the day of decision. The moment of truth was at hand.

chapter 14

The Wednesday-morning mail brought the final autopsy report from San Bernardino, just in time to suit Virgil's purposes. He tore open the thick official envelope and studied the grim contents thoroughly.

When he had been over the report twice, he picked up a pad of paper and sketched the outlines of a human figure in both front and profile views. Then he carefully shaded in the areas where, according to the autopsy, the body had received blows. When he had finished, he had a reasonably accurate picture of the beating the dead chemist had received, with those particular areas that had contributed specifically to his death outlined in red.

Satisfied with his work, he phoned Michael Wolfram, the attorney. When he had the lawyer on the line, he came right to the point.

"Mr. Wolfram, knowing that you represent Walter Mc-Cormack, and that he and the late Dr. Roussel were both close friends and business associates, it occurred to me that you might also have handled Dr. Roussel's legal business in this country."

"You're quite right," Wolfram acknowledged. "What can I do for you?"

Tibbs made an appointment for eleven-thirty and hung up.

After glancing through the rest of his mail, which was unimportant, he left the office and picked up one of the official cars that carry the special equipment used by the Investigative Division and drove it southward from the Pasadena civic center.

On the way down the Arroyo Seco toward the freeway, an ancient car with the front end dipped significantly down pulled illegally close behind him. Virgil glanced into the mirror and saw that the two occupants were boys, neither of whom appeared old enough to have a driving license. In a few seconds the car whipped out, drew alongside him, and then pulled to a stop at a red light. The boy on the right leaned out and slapped the side of the door.

"Come on, black boy!" he shouted. "Let's see if you can go."

When the light changed, the old car jumped forward, burning rubber on the dry concrete. As soon as it was ahead, the driver swung it recklessly close in front of the unmarked police car and hit the brakes. Virgil knew the maneuver and was ready; having already checked that there was no other traffic, he cut sharply to the left and then, reaching down, touched the control for the concealed siren under the hood. He did not allow it to come up to speed; he sounded it only enough so that the other driver would recognize what it was.

At once the dragsters became ultra-respectable; their old car moved into the right-hand lane and sedately held to the legal speed limit. As Virgil drove past, he looked carefully at the driver and checked the license plate against the hot sheet that is issued daily by the Los Angeles Police Department. Then he picked up the radio mike.

Within four blocks a motorcycle officer appeared at a traffic light and fell in behind the modified car. The situation under control, Virgil cleared the green light at the beginning of the freeway and came up to speed. He relaxed during the fifteen minutes it took him to reach the four-level interchange, and then continued on straight through down the Harbor Freeway until he reached Olympic, where he turned off and headed westward. Within a minute or two he pulled up across the street from a sign that read "ALL AMERICA KARATE FEDERATION" and flipped down the visor that would identify the car to any police officer. He got out and walked into the building.

The Nisei at the front counter looked up and registered mild surprise. "Hello, Virgil, didn't expect you."

"Is Sensei* here?" Tibbs asked.

"Just changing. You can catch him in the locker room."

Virgil walked down the short corridor past the exercise rooms and the main training area and turned into the dressing room. In his hand he held the sketches he had made before leaving his office.

In the Spartan but efficient locker room there were two men, both of whom were knotting black belts as Tibbs came in. The one nearer to him was a Japanese of medium height and apparently light build, although the white training *gi* he was wearing concealed the outlines of his physique. He was in his mid-thirties and obviously charged with a high level of controlled nervous energy. As Virgil walked in, he looked up and flashed a smile.

"Good morning, Virgil," he said with a perceptible accent.

"Good morning, Sensei." Tibbs shook hands with both men

---

* A Japanese term that combines the meanings of "teacher" and "master." A corresponding word is the Italian "maestro."

and produced his sketches. Then he hesitated. The man to whom he wanted to speak had a limited command of English, and he did not wish to risk giving offense. Since the second man was a Nisei, he solved the problem by explaining the problem to them both. He gave a brief account of the murder and pointed out the significant areas in the drawings.

His diplomacy was successful. The man he had addressed as Sensei examined the drawings carefully and asked several questions of his companion in rapid staccato Japanese. They were answered just as fluently, and what was clearly a technical discussion continued for some time. Then the Nisei turned to Tibbs.

"Nishiyama Sensei would like to know the exact height and weight of the dead man, if you have that information."

Virgil supplied the figures from memory; Nishiyama nodded again quickly and once more consulted the drawings. Then the karate master shook his head.

"It was not a karate man," he explained. Continuing in English, he began a technical description that Tibbs listened to attentively. Although he was himself highly trained in the art, he knew that he could not match his knowledge against that of a world authority. The essence of Nishiyama's opinion was that the killer had been well schooled in no-holds-barred street fighting and had attained reasonable proficiency, but he did not know karate. The master based his conclusions not only on the nature of the blows the body had received but also on the number. A competent karate man would not have required the quantity shown.

Tibbs thanked him warmly and declined an invitation to remain and train for a period of what Nishiyama chose to call light sparring. He had sparred with Nishiyama before, and despite what he had learned from the session, he was in no immediate hurry to repeat the experience.

Armed with the information, which had confirmed his own opinion, Virgil returned to his car and set out for his appointment with the attorney. His case was now very nearly complete, but for that very reason he was determined to overlook no detail that might later prove to be significant.

When he reached the attorney's office, Wolfram received him and motioned him to a chair. He proved to be an unexpectedly small man whose immaculate, expensive suit contrasted with his bushy, undisciplined hair. Tibbs noted that all the furniture in the office was scaled down to minimize the slight stature of Wolfram, who looked more like a successful retired jockey than a power in the courtroom.

After the amenities, Virgil outlined the case, concerning which the attorney was already partially informed. As he neared the end of his recital, Wolfram interrupted. "Mr. Tibbs," he asked, "are you coming to the point of telling me that one of my clients is in jeopardy?"

"No," Virgil answered. "At least not at this time. Of course, I don't know your client roster, so I couldn't answer that question in any event. Actually I'm here for information."

Wolfram nodded. "Please go on."

"When are you going to submit Dr. Roussel's will for probate?"

"Almost immediately—in fact, today."

"Would you have any serious objection if I asked you to postpone doing so for, say, twenty-four hours?"

Wolfram leaned back and suddenly, despite his small size, looked remarkably shrewd and responsible. "Would you care to give me a reason?" he asked.

"I'm after someone. Delaying the publication of the will might help me to get him."

"I see. In that case I'll go along with you. Anything else?"

"Yes," Virgil answered. "I'd like to read the will, if I may. One provision it may contain would interest me very much."

"Is this an official request?"

"Definitely."

Wolfram drew his legs up and hung his heels on the edge of his chair. "If it will help to pin the guilt on Al Roussel's murderer, I'm for it," he said. "On general principles I'd suggest that you keep it to yourself as much as you can."

"Agreed," Tibbs answered.

Wolfram pressed a button. When a secretary responded, he said simply, "The Roussel will," and then they waited. As soon as the document arrived, he handed it to Tibbs.

As Virgil turned the long legal pages with the numbered lines, only the rustling of the paper broke the silence. In five minutes he had finished and handed the will back. "Thank you," he said.

"Any time." The lawyer looked at him. "Are you getting at all close? Or can't you tell me?"

Tibbs got to his feet. "It shouldn't be too long," he answered.

Returning downtown, he stopped at the Los Angeles Police Department, but the man he wanted to see had gone to lunch. While he waited, he had his usual sandwich and a malted at a lunch counter and pondered what he had learned that morning.

162   *

Having built up his case, he tried to tear it down again in his own mind, but this time it appeared to hold water. He realized that he would have to take a calculated risk and play for a break, since he had no witnesses and the concrete evidence he had assembled might or might not be enough to convince a jury. Before the day was over, he would either have it made or be in deep trouble. He refused to worry. If he did his part properly, as he had planned, the rest should take care of itself.

By the time he had finished his eating and his mental review, the police expert in rough-and-tumble street fighting was back and available. Once more Virgil produced his sketches and asked some very specific questions. After making detailed notes he knew that an additional important piece had been fitted into place. For the first time he was confident that he knew almost the whole story.

At that point another thought crossed his mind and he phoned the home of Mrs. Joyce Pratt. The owner was not there, but the intelligent Negro maid he had met on his first visit was quite willing to talk to him. She apologized for the unfortunate tea episode, and Tibbs reassured her with the information that hot tea was something he disliked. The conversation continued for some time, during which the maid succeeded in learning that Tibbs was unmarried and Virgil in turn picked up a few pieces of information he found equally interesting.

While he was thus engaged, certain other events began to shape themselves without his knowledge. George Nunn called Pine Shadows Lodge to repeat his invitation for that evening; better prepared this time, Ellen Boardman accepted.

Officer Dick Mooney privately phoned headquarters and

reported that everything was quiet at the lodge and that there was no evidence of any kind of trouble.

Oswald Peterson, the broker, was served with formal papers informing him that his estranged wife was upping her demands for alimony in connection with her suit for divorce on the grounds of adultery.

William Holt-Rymers had a private telephone conversation with Walter McCormack during which Virgil Tibbs was freely discussed.

Joyce Pratt called Michael Wolfram and asked a number of questions to which she did not receive satisfactory answers; at least they did not satisfy her.

Arthur Greenberg, of the optical company, had a confidential discussion with Dr. Nathan Shapiro concerning a certain irregular prescription.

Mike Casella, the construction contractor, left his office on what he announced would be an inspection trip and added that he would not be back before the first of the following week.

One more item remained on Virgil's list of things to do— a single last detail that he wanted to check. He called at the West Coast offices of a major corporation, glanced at the lobby board, and took the elevator to the executive offices. He stepped out into an aura of thick carpeting, rich wood paneling, and a studied quiet. A perfectly groomed and carefully detached receptionist looked up and awarded him an official meaningless smile, which implied that he was of course welcome, but only up to a point unless he had business of genuine importance.

Tibbs presented his card and stated that he would like to see Mr. Emil Weidler, the vice-president in charge.

The receptionist picked up a phone and dialed three digits.

"Mr. Virgil Tibbs, of the Pasadena Police Department, is here to see you," she reported. "He is an investigator."

She listened for a moment and replaced the instrument.

"Mr. Weidler suggests that you contact Mr. Hennessey in the legal department." She penciled a number on a slip of paper and handed it to Tibbs. "You can take the elevator to your right."

Virgil sighed inwardly. The moats and armor of medieval times had their counterpart in the modern industrial buffer-receptionist.

"Perhaps I failed to make myself clear," he said without changing the level of his voice. "This is an official call. I wish to see Mr. Weidler and no one else."

The girl looked at him, clearly trying to measure the amount of authority behind his words. Then, reluctantly, she once more picked up the phone; the official smile was gone. After a brief conversation she became cool and efficient.

"Mr. Weidler will see you—the second door on the right."

That was better; Virgil went down the thickly carpeted corridor and opened the heavy wood door that had been designated. It was not marked.

Weidler was medium-height, in his late forties, and at least twenty pounds overweight. He wore his hair plastered back in a style that was wrong for his round, rather pushed-in face. He looked up, but did not rise, as Tibbs entered.

"Oh," he said in some surprise. "Are *you* the police officer?"

"I am," Virgil replied and sat down without waiting to be asked. He was suddenly tired of being looked at like some kind of freak; if people didn't care to show him reasonable courtesy, then he saw no need to go out of his way to stand on ceremony with them.

"I believe you knew Dr. Albert Roussel."

"I met him once," Weidler replied. "But I knew his work certainly."

"I'm investigating his murder," Tibbs said, keeping the advantage. "It is most important that I know certain details concerning your company's offer to buy out the holders of his patents. I assume you are fully acquainted with the facts."

Weidler became cautious. "This is a very delicate and confidential matter—" he began.

Virgil cut him off. "Mr. Weidler, I don't want to appear discourteous, but at this moment time is very important. I already know most of the facts, but I need a few more immediately. Let me remind you that this is a murder investigation. If you don't care to confide in me now, you may have to do your talking later, publicly, on the witness stand."

Weidler pulled out a handkerchief and wiped it across his flat face. "What do you want to know?" he asked.

"Now that Dr. Roussel is dead, are you still interested in acquiring the rights to his patents?"

"Yes."

"How valuable are they?"

Weidler hesitated briefly. "Very valuable. We've been paying royalties on them for years."

"Without them would you be able to continue your basic color-film production as at present?"

"No." The tone of Weidler's voice changed. "May I see your credentials, please?"

Tibbs produced them.

"Is this confidential?" Weidler asked.

"As far as possible."

"All right, then, it amounts to this. For a great many years we have maintained a very strong position in the amateur photography field. Now our principal competition has come up with a new film that has us beat. It's faster, has better color definition, and an almost invisible grain. Amateurs can process it themselves fairly easily, and we lose both the revenue from the sale of the film and the laboratory work."

Virgil nodded. "I know. I've used the film and it's excellent."

Weidler lowered his voice. "Before he died, Dr. Roussel came up with something that will allow us to compete. This is very *sub rosa*." He paused to be sure the statement had sunk in. "Our competition found out about it and have been negotiating for the process. We must have it or we will lose our control of much of the market."

"What if the Roussel stockholders decide not to sell?"

Weidler pursed his lips. "I think they will," he said finally. "We have made a very attractive offer and they are not very big people."

"But if they don't?"

"Then we will have to resort to other measures. Reluctantly, of course."

Virgil left with a distaste for Weidler and for the company he represented, but he did not have time to concern himself with the maneuvers and power politics of big business. He had the information he wanted and he was almost ready to put it to use.

He phoned the home of Joyce Pratt and was told that

madam would not be in until evening and then she would be entertaining. Walter McCormack was also out and his household did not know when he would return.

Oswald Peterson had not been in his office all day; his secretary reported he was out of town.

Stymied for the moment, Tibbs drove back to Pasadena, cleared his desk of several minor matters, and laid his plans for the evening. Then, to compose himself, he drove his own car to a nearby Japanese restaurant. Shoes off, he sat on a straw tatami mat before a low table and watched as the kimono-clad waitress knelt and prepared sukiyaki for him over an electric stove.

The quiet dignity of the restaurant and the change of atmosphere were exactly what he needed to relax the coiled springs he had carried within himself most of the day.

Just before eight, back at his office, he picked up the phone and called the Los Angeles Police Department.

"I'm coming into your jurisdiction," he advised, and arranged for a Los Angeles plainclothes officer to meet him, as proper police courtesy required. It was the only way the several law-enforcement bodies in the Los Angeles basin could keep track of what was happening in their respective territories.

At a little after eight-thirty Tibbs pulled off the freeway and winked the lights of the official car he was driving as he came down the ramp. A black Chevrolet parked at the bottom winked in reply and Virgil pulled up alongside.

"Virgil Tibbs, Pasadena," he introduced himself.

The Los Angeles officer was youngish, pleasant, but with the square-jawed look of a man who could handle himself. "Frank Sims, Mr. Tibbs. I've heard of you. What's up?"

"I'm going to pick up a murder suspect. Remember the body that was found in the nudist park?"

"I sure do. How can I help?"

"I'm not certain yet, but it may get a little rough. The person I want to take may put up a pretty determined fight."

"I've heard you're a karate black belt."

"Yes, I am."

"Then I don't see the problem. I'm not at that level yet, but I'm pretty well up in aikido. And, of course, in the rough-and-tumble stuff, if it comes to that."

"Then you don't mind? You see, I'd rather keep a show of guns out of this, if I can."

"I'm with you."

"Then let's go. We have two stops to make."

"Lead the way."

Virgil swung his car around and headed west. The Chevrolet fell in behind him and followed smoothly with the sure control of an expert driver. The small procession moved into the exclusive residential area west of Beverly Hills, turned into the Bel Air entrance, and after a few blocks of winding drive pulled up before the residence of Mrs. Joyce Pratt. Virgil parked and joined Frank Sims on the curb.

"I don't expect we will be especially welcome here," he warned, "but I'd appreciate it if you would come along just the same."

He looked at the house, which blazed with light on the lower floor; then with Sims beside him he walked quietly to the front door and pushed the bell.

The Negro maid answered, looked at him under the porch light, and said, "Good evening, Mr. Tibbs."

Virgil gave her good marks for remembering his name.

"Mr. Sims and I would like to see Mrs. Pratt," he said. "I know that she is entertaining, but it is a matter of the greatest importance."

The maid showed them into the small foyer and then went into the living room, where Virgil could see her as she bent over to speak quietly to her mistress. Joyce Pratt was out of his line of vision, but he heard her clearly when she spoke. "Impossible! He has no business here at this hour. Tell him I cannot be disturbed and that I do not appreciate his visit."

Frank Sims nudged Virgil in the ribs. Resigning himself to what he had to do. Tibbs glanced toward the Los Angeles officer, motioned him to follow, and then walked uninvited into the living room.

He found himself more or less face to face with sixteen people seated around four bridge tables. Two of them were semi-elderly men; the rest were women. All of them stopped what they had been doing and silence gripped the room.

"Mr. Tibbs, you are not welcome. I must ask you to leave." It was an angry command; her guests were watching with rapt attention.

Virgil spoke quietly, so quietly that not everyone present heard him. "Mrs. Pratt, I must have a word with you in private at once. It is urgent. I'm sure your guests will excuse you."

"*Mr.* Tibbs, leave this house!" Her eyes blazed and the muscles of her small body tightened into rigidity.

"You leave me no choice; I had hoped to spare you." Tibbs kept his own voice quiet and controlled. "Mrs. Pratt, I am placing you under arrest for the murder of Albert Roussel. It will be necessary for you to come with me. Your maid will get your wrap."

chapter 15

The small woman sat motionless, the muscles of her face held under taut control. When she spoke, her voice seemed to be caught in her throat.

"Mr. Tibbs, you are demented."

"I fear not, Mrs. Pratt," he replied. "If you engage people to perform murders for you, then you share their guilt and must face the consequences."

"I don't know what you're talking about." Each word was wrapped in its own icy shroud.

"In the eyes of the law, *you* are a murderer," Tibbs answered. "I know the person you hired to do your murder. I also know when and why. Now I suggest that we put off any further discussion. In light of recent court decisions, I strongly recommend that you phone your attorney from our booking room and have him advise you concerning your rights."

Joyce Pratt closed her tiny hands into fists and slammed them down against the table top. She half rose from her chair, uncontrolled fury in her eyes, and shook her head violently as though to drive a frightful apparition away.

"Get out of my house!" she shouted. "Get out of my home!" Tears began to run from the corners of her eyes.

"After you, Mrs. Pratt," Virgil said.

Like a berserk doll, Joyce Pratt turned on Tibbs and hammered against his chest with her fists. In her frenzy she forgot where she was, forgot those around her, forgot everything but the rage that consumed her. She screamed at him with words that defamed him, his manhood, and his ancestry—vicious and reckless words, violent and profane.

Frank Sims reached out firmly and shook her. "That's enough," he snapped. He took her by the elbow and turned her toward the door.

But Joyce was still not through. "I'll kill you, you black bastard!" she screamed at Tibbs. "You can't prove a word of it."

Virgil felt a surge of vindication. He had known he was right, but his confidence was strengthened by her unintended confession. He knew, as every experienced policeman does, that the words "You can't prove" are spoken only by the guilty.

The maid appeared, almost amazingly composed, with Joyce Pratt's wrap across her arm. She remained poker-faced as Frank Sims took it and put it across her mistress's shoulders. Sims, too, had heard her declaration and knew that she was guilty.

Joyce threw back her head and began to laugh, a wild senseless laugh that echoed obscenely through the room.

"You're too late," she cried, laughing at Tibbs. "You can't help them *now*. I'm way ahead of you!"

Her voice broke and she began to sob hysterically.

Virgil looked at her a moment; then his body stiffened. "Take her, Frank," he barked, and whirled toward the door. He jerked it open and raced across the lawn toward his waiting car on the dead run.

He was hardly behind the wheel when he hit the ignition,

caught the opening cough of the engine, and snapped on the radio. He already knew that there was little if anything that he could do, but the thing he had failed to foresee compelled him to attempt everything possible. The moment he had power, he pulled the car into a tight U turn, flipped on the red spotlight, and hit the concealed siren.

In Code 3 condition he made Sunset Boulevard in less than two minutes, turned, and headed for the San Diego Freeway. He drove with one hand, holding the microphone in the other. When he reached the overpass, he turned north through the Santa Monica Mountains, a maneuver that would put him on the Ventura Freeway down the backbone of the San Fernando Valley. On the freeway he turned off the siren, knowing that he would gain nothing in speed and only cause accidents—a lesson the fire department had learned a long time ago.

It took him eight minutes at top speed to clear the pass and turn eastward, at last on the wide pavement of the Ventura Freeway. He pushed his speed up to past eighty in the far left lane and waited, his body alert and tense, for word from the radio dispatcher.

He was on a wild-goose chase and knew it, but he could not restrain himself. There were many others to do the work for him, but his own involvement was such that nothing could have held him back.

As he crossed Coldwater Canyon, the first report came in; Dick Mooney had been spoken to at Pine Shadows Lodge and had advised that everything was quiet. Ellen Boardman was out on a date with George Nunn.

Virgil had expected that; he kept his foot hard on the gas pedal and glanced once more at the gasoline gauge. He had already checked the gauge four times since reaching the freeway (the car, as always, had been filled before he had taken it out), but his suppressed body demanded action and that was one small thing he could do.

He was so intent on his driving that he did not see the motorcycle until the officer riding it, young and determined, motioned him to the side. Instead Virgil reached down and touched the siren control. As soon as he heard the sound, the motorcycle man quickly nodded his head and pointed forward. Tibbs raised his left hand in a quick greeting and sped on.

He had reached the Golden State Freeway before the second report came in: Ellen Boardman and George Nunn were not at Sun Valley Lodge; the Nunns knew that they were out together, but had no idea where they had gone.

A huge truck-trailer loomed in the way and began to change lanes ahead of the speeding police car. Cursing under his breath, Virgil cut sharply to his left directly in front of a white Oldsmobile, which was doing a legally proper sixty-five. The driver blasted his horn and almost swerved into the divider. Once more Virgil touched the siren enough to let the outraged driver know that it was a police car, the only apology he could make.

At the speed he was traveling, the red spotlight still on, he was soon at the San Bernardino Freeway intersection. Reluctantly he slowed down to negotiate the interchange ramp and then picked up speed once more when he was again headed east. Despite the several curves and a moderate flow of traffic, he steadied himself behind the wheel and cut the miles away as he waited for the radio to speak.

Again he remembered that he could do little or nothing;

his mad dash to a destination still more than an hour away was close to recklessness. He had already set in motion, via radio, all the law-enforcement agencies on hand in the San Bernardino area and they were good and capable men. But like a man pursued by furies he drove himself, and the car he was in, to the limit of his ability.

He was climbing out of the Los Angeles basin over the ridge when a first report came through from the San Bernardino Sheriff's Department: George Nunn's car had not been spotted in the area; a thorough check was being continued.

The speedometer of the police car touched and passed eighty-five as Virgil came down the eastern side of the ridge and plunged on toward Ontario and Fontana. His fingers opened and closed as he gripped the wheel; he cut his way through traffic and past angry drivers who looked in their rear-view mirrors hoping to see a cop.

A rebuilt Mercury blowing smoke from its exhaust pulled alongside to race. This time Virgil did not bother to use the siren; he sped on and left the Mercury behind.

He passed Ontario and dropped his speed of necessity when the road narrowed down to two lanes. He cut past a diesel truck that blocked his way and ignored the flashing lights the driver threw into his mirror. At Fontana he took the left-lane cutoff and once more turned on the siren. Ignoring the stop signs, he was on Route 66 eastbound in less than eight minutes, the Kaiser Steel Works vanishing behind him. He turned off and headed toward the mountains.

Traffic fell to nothing and he stopped the siren. Now he heard the rush of the wind and the whine of the tires against the hard roadway, and felt the heat of the desert as he drew nearer to the El Cajon Pass. The headlights bit tunnels in the darkness while the moonlight gave him the rough contour of the ground ahead. His body ached from the tension building in it, but now that he was almost where he wanted desperately to be, he could not relax for an instant. He expected at any moment to encounter a patrolling police car, but apparently none had been assigned to this back-road cutoff.

In a few minutes he reached the base of the mountain and began to climb. He had had a great deal of time to think and his mind told him the place to go. Every other likely spot would be covered; a patrol car was waiting silently at Ellen Boardman's home and another was stationed just outside Sun Valley Lodge. Only one place remained unguarded, and when he thought of it, Virgil felt a freezing stab of fear.

"It's such a lovely evening," Ellen Boardman said.

"It is indeed." George Nunn swung the car moderately and easily around the broad switchback and fed a little more gas as a six-percent climb came into view. The engine throbbed as it attacked the grade and felt the strain of the thinning air. When they had reached the top of the ascent and the road curved to climb once more, George swung the wheel the opposite way and turned off onto the level parking area at the high viewpoint. As he stopped the engine and carefully set the hand brake, he could already see the fantastic blanket of light spread over the silent land more than a mile below.

Ellen turned to him and smiled, letting him know that she approved his stopping here at her favorite turnout. George opened the door and helped her out. As he did so, he saw there was another car parked well down at the extreme edge of the turnout; the people in it, he decided, had chosen that spot because they did not wish to be disturbed. Then he dismissed them from his mind.

He and Ellen walked to the edge and stood, hand in hand, silently absorbing the wide panorama of tens of thousands of lights challenging the growing blackness of the night. George let his fingers tighten a little and was enraptured when a slight pressure came in return.

He did not see the dark shadow that was approaching; he heard no sound. His mind, and his whole being, were concentrated on the girl beside him; in just a moment he was going to take her in his arms. Then he turned to her and with sudden shock saw that they were not alone. He looked up and into the face of evil.

He gulped a quick breath and knew.

He knew who and what it was, and he knew that he would have to fight—probably for his life and for that of the girl, who now looked up startled, not knowing why his hands had suddenly gone as hard as iron.

He turned Ellen around away from him, faced the big man, and said, "Yes?"

For one moment he took hope when he saw no weapon; at the same time he heard the quick, frightened gasp from Ellen that told him she knew, too.

By the moonlight he saw the man he guessed to be a murderer draw back his lips and reveal his white clenched teeth. Then all hope vanished as the man raised his hands and advanced.

George took a bare second to wonder if he would have time to peel off his coat to free his arms for what they must do. At once he knew it would be fatal and instead raised his own arms in a boxing stance. He was not much of a boxer, but a sudden surge of reckless determination gave him courage. At the first attack he would block with his left and cross with his right, to the point of the jaw if he could make it.

The big man lunged at him, fastened one huge hand around his left wrist, and with the other thrust forward seized George's throat.

With all his power George pounded his right fist into the man's ribs. He hit so hard his knuckles seemed to shatter, but the blow had no effect. The thumb of the attacker's left hand pressed into the triangle at the base of George's throat and pain seemed to paralyze his whole body.

Then he heard Ellen scream and saw her dash herself against the impossibly big man. Holding one of her shoes in her hand, she tried futilely to beat the heel against his skull.

The attacker released his grip on George's throat and with his free arm swept the girl aside as he might have thrust a sappling out of the way. He caught her across the breasts and she fell backward sharply, landing hard on her back in the loose gravel.

Then, remembering a trick he had heard about, George gathered all the strength he could muster and snapped his knee hard toward the man's groin. He had almost reached his target when the powerful leg muscles of the other man's body tightened and trapped George's leg in a massive vise.

Then two hands seized George's throat and fingers locked behind his head. His leg was freed, but his head was snapped downward with commanding force; he saw the raised knee just before his face was smashed against the hard area above the attacker's kneecap, and he slid to the ground mercifully unconscious.

A flash of distant light touched the mountain opposite the parking area and the sound of a car coming could be heard in the still night.

The attacker, looming huge and dark against the sky, aimed a swift, vicious kick to George's ribs; then he flung himself on the ground beside Ellen and clasped his huge hand over her mouth and face.

As a last, hopeless, desperate resort she had hoped to reason with him, to beg for mercy if she must, but now she had to fight hard just to breathe. Before her there swam the bright-red image of her helpless escort and the realization that the horror of rape was upon her. She tried to kick her feet and twist away, but the powerful clamp across her face tightened mercilessly and she was forced to be still.

The car came nearer, fighting the steep grade at the limit of its power. The lights reached the crest of the hill, swung across the surface of the parking area, and found the three people sprawled motionless on the ground. The car came rushing toward them as though to destroy them under its wheels; then it swerved and the acrid smell of burning rubber filled the air as it screamed to a stop.

In a single bound the attacker was on his feet; he charged the car and thrust his powerful arm through the open window to grab the man behind the wheel.

As the attack came, Tibbs rolled sharply across the seat, yanked the right-hand door open, thrust out his feet, and gained the ground.

With the first lungful of air she could gather, Ellen cried, "Watch out!" Virgil did not need the warning, but it told him that she was probably all right, and that he was still in time. He shot a quick glance at George, who lay motionless face down; even in the cold stillness of the moonlight he could see that he was gone—unconscious or dead. It gave him complete justification for what he had to do. Then there was no more time as the big man appeared before him.

Tibbs knew that he was outweighed by more than sixty pounds as he faced the man who recognized him as a mortal enemy. He made a deliberate effort to control his breathing and to relax the tenseness in his body so that he could move with maximum speed. As he had been trained to do for many years, he waited for the other man to make the first move.

It came swiftly and without warning. The huge man whirled sidewise and aimed a vicious kick at the small of Tibbs' back. As the leg came through the air, Virgil spun to his left to meet it. In a sharp movement he dropped his body down, his left leg bent, knee outward, and his right leg thrust hard against the ground. Holding the greater part of his weight on the muscle below his left knee—in the karate stance known as *zenkutsu-dachi*—he whipped his left arm up in front of his body, elbow bent and fist clenched, and braced it with his right fist against the inside of his elbow. As the impact of the attacker's leg hit the block, pain shot through Tibbs' arm, but the force of the kick was shattered.

Countering instantly, Virgil locked his arms across his chest as though he were hugging himself and snapped his right elbow with concerted force into the attacker's lower floating ribs.

The big man jerked out an animal sound as the blow hit him, but he smashed a massive fist at Tibbs' abdomen. With all his might Virgil whipped his left arm down and took the impact wrist to wrist, sweeping the other man's fist away from his body. Then, having the advantage for a split second, he leaned to the left, raised his right foot knee high, and aimed a roundhouse kick at his opponent's armpit.

The big man had been trained, too; he blocked with his great forearm and jerked up a knee thrust at Virgil's groin. Because he had snapped his right leg back as fast as it had gone forward, Virgil kept his balance and thrust his left knee forward to divert the blow. He was not sparring now; it was deadly, and with no quarter asked or given. Knowing this, he planted his right foot with the knee bent and aimed a side-thrust kick with his left leg, using all the speed he could command. He felt the outer edge of his foot smash against the rib cage of his opponent and knew that the power behind it had gone home.

Despite the cool night air his lungs fought to breathe, his shirt clung to his back, and great beads of perspiration stood out on his forehead. His left wrist surged with pain where he had blocked the blow aimed at his abdomen. He desperately needed his second wind, but it had not yet come.

For a moment both men stopped, face to face, each aware that the other was trained and hardened—one in the violence of street fighting, the other in the deadly, ultra-refined techniques of karate. Virgil did not let the pause deceive him; he sank down even lower into front stance with his left leg forward, and by the faint light watched the other man's eyes, because that would be the place where the first warning would be flashed.

He saw the flicker before the fist shot out and snapped up a rising block with his left hand. If the blow was a feint, he was ready, but it was in earnest. He turned forty-five degrees with his body, keeping his feet still and swinging from his hips. Then, instantly, he realized that the huge man had made the first mistake—his abdomen was exposed.

Virgil shot out his left arm, not to strike but to provide re-coil force. With his body loose he whipped his arm back, spun his hips until they faced the attacker, and to this concentrated force added the power of his shoulders as they, too, snapped around in front-on position. The combination hip-and-shoulder movement, coupled with the recoil of his left arm, shot Virgil's right arm out with whiplash force. He kept the attack straight, his elbows close to his body, his right fist traveling in a direct line to the midpoint in front of his own body.

At the last instant before impact, he tightened his entire body—legs, hips, torso, shoulders, and arm—and his fist smashed home with the total concentrated power of his trained muscles.

The deadly *gyaku-zuki* reverse punch caught the big man in the vital spot just below his breastbone. Because of its sheer power, it penetrated below his tensed and hardened muscles and forced him to jackknife his body to absorb the impact. As the man's head came down, Virgil jerked up his right hand, open and rigid, in a slight S curve, and whipped it down with an elbow snap onto the side of the neck.

It was a fearful blow delivered with total precision. The man went down, apparently still, a heap of flesh and bone, the viciousness run out of him like water from a broken jar. Virgil stood, sweat running into his eyes, his lungs gasping for air, his chest pounding with pain. He thought he might have finished the fight, but he was not sure and could take no chances.

He did not take his eyes from the fallen man as Ellen rushed past him and dropped to her knees beside the still figure of George Nunn. Virgil felt a stickiness between his fingers and knew that his hands were bleeding. Meanwhile Ellen had turned George over and was gently pressing a handkerchief against his bloodied face.

"Someone is coming," Virgil said without turning. "I called them."

She looked up at him and her lips moved, but she could form no words. For a moment he glanced at her, and it nearly cost him his life. From the apparently inert man on the ground an arm shot out toward his ankle. Virgil jerked his knee up barely in time, then thrust his leg downward like a ramrod, his foot turned so that the outer edge would strike. He felt the ribs smash under the impact and knew then that he could be sure the fight was over.

Ellen began to cry. She sat back on her heels and her body shook with sobs. Virgil looked once more at the inert man on the ground and then walked over to where George lay. He dropped to his knees opposite Ellen, laid his head against George's chest, and listened to his breathing.

"He's banged up a little," Virgil said, "but I think he'll be all right. He's good and sturdy."

At last Ellen found her voice. "He tried so hard," she sobbed.

In the stillness that followed, they both heard the sound of a racing engine echoing in the air. It was well down the mountain, but it was coming fast.

There was a first-aid kit in the police car, but Virgil thought it best to wait; the people coming expected trouble and would have an ambulance with them. The sound grew louder.

"Did you—kill him?" Ellen asked and looked toward the man who lay still a few feet away.

"I don't think so," Virgil answered her. "That last was the worst, but it had to be done."

"I know," she agreed.

A low, incoherent sound came from George's lips, like the escape of air from a tight container. Ellen bent and kissed him, unmindful of the dirt, the streaks of blood, or the man who was watching.

The oncoming vehicle reached the bottom of the grade and was now on the final climb; the loom of its headlights showed against the wall of the mountain.

Ellen looked at Virgil. "If you hadn't come—" she began, and could go no further.

"My pleasure," he said. The understatement seemed to fit the situation. His hands stung with pain, his left wrist was agonizing, and the sharp stabbing hurt would not leave his lungs. He had not yet recovered his wind and his body was fighting to readjust itself.

George's left hand twitched against the ground. Ellen raised his head gently and held it, not knowing quite what to do. Virgil realized that he still had his coat on; he took it off, folded it into a pillow, and slid it under George's head.

The sound was almost upon them now and the lights of the vehicle were bright against the sky.

"Who is—that terrible man?" Ellen asked. She forced herself to look again toward the still shape on the ground.

Virgil rose unsteadily to his feet. "The only one it could be," he answered wearily. Suddenly the fierce tension that had been driving him for the past two hours was gone, and he could hardly control his own movements. "Only one man knew enough and thought he had a motive."

The lights of the sheriff's car hit him as he stood there in his shirt sleeves, his energy spent.

"You saw him once before, I think, when he came to your place. His name is Brown—Walter Brown. Among other things he's Walter McCormack's chauffeur."

chapter 16

The warm, radiant California sun hung in high glory in the sky and presented the land underneath with a day that not even the native sons could exaggerate. The weather was so splendid that Mrs. Mary Agnew forsook the usual isolation of her rural living room and seated herself on her front lawn, where she could be certain of missing no detail of what went on.

When a conspicuously marked police car drove quietly past, her heart took a quick leap; at long last they were going to raid that nudist colony down the road! She was disconcerted that there was only one car, but it was a beginning. She hoped with a devout passion that they would drag out that blond girl, screaming, and take her away to the city to be a public spectacle.

Mrs. Agnew had a mind shaped like a keyhole. For many years now she had devoted her life almost exclusively to the relentless scrutiny of everything within her range of vision. It was her tightly locked secret that though she had never been married, she had borne a child at eighteen; from that moment she had dedicated herself to learning everything possible about the faults of the rest of mankind. To her the existence of nudists, not only on the same planet but within a mile radius of her chosen home, was almost unbearable. She literally lived for the glorious day when hordes of official vehicles would descend upon the evil place and the fate of Sodom would be re-enacted. The police car gave her a quickened hope and she leaned forward to listen—to hear, if possible, if it would turn into the driveway of That Place.

To her exquisite delight, it did.

Mrs. Agnew, contrary to her usual form, had missed a detail: she had not seen the person behind the wheel. If she had, her inventive mind would have conjured up incredible possibilities concerning his presence at the nudist resort. Mrs. Agnew coughed, and remembered that she had forgotten to take her digitalis.

Virgil Tibbs drove smoothly through the S turn and parked the police car in a corner of the big lot nearest the house. As he got out and stood for a moment in thought, he heard the bright optimism of the unseen birds in the trees and, from the direction of the pool area, the laughing, splashing sounds of children in the water.

He began to walk toward the converted farmhouse and encountered Carole; he had to look twice to recognize her in clothes.

"Hello, Virgil," she said, and rushed up to make him welcome.

"Hello, Carole." He held out his hand. The soft pressure of her fingers did not reopen the pain of his raw knuckles and he suddenly felt peaceful and very much at home.

"I made Linda promise I could meet you," Carole confided. She walked close beside him to the door of the big kitchen. Forrest Nunn met them at the steps and greeted him warmly.

"Thank you," he said simply, "for what you did for my

son." Perhaps it was the intonation of "my son" that made his few words eloquent.

"I'm glad I was there," Virgil answered. Between the two men there was no need for more explanation.

Emily was just inside the door and to Tibbs' surprise there were tears in her eyes. She took his scarred hands in her own. "Virgil, what can I say to you?" she asked.

"George did fine," he said casually. "I came along in time to finish up the job, that's all."

Emily shook her head from side to side and pressed her lips together. "Do come in," she murmured. It was all she could say.

There was quite a group in the kitchen. Ellen Boardman was there, sitting next to George at the table; apart from the bandage on his forehead and the strap of adhesive tape across his nose, he looked quite normal.

William Holt-Rymers sat, clad in sandals and the briefest of swim trunks, before a littered ash tray and a cup of coffee.

Only Linda was missing, but in a sense she was there, too. In the corner of the room, easel-mounted, there was an unframed canvas that had captured in oils and brush strokes such glowing and brilliant light that it seemed to be radiant. In the painted greens, yellows, and browns of the grove of trees near the pool there was beauty and serene power, but they were eclipsed by the radiant likeness of the head and shoulders of Linda. She seemed to be transformed into some exalted symbol of all young womanhood, from her clear-blue unafraid eyes to her firm, beautifully formed breasts. It was a wonderful picture.

Virgil turned to Holt-Rymers. "It's magnificent," he said.

The artist shrugged. "You catch murderers," he said. "I paint."

"Linda is down at the pool teaching the junior swim class," Carole said. "She'll be up any time now."

Virgil looked once more at the picture in admiration. He would have given everything he possessed to be able to create a thing of beauty like it. No photograph could do what the portrait did; no film could create the things that Holt-Rymers had put in the painting.

"We'll be ready as soon as Linda is through and dressed," Emily said. "It won't take her long. Please have some coffee."

Virgil sat down and accepted the hospitality. "How are you feeling, Miss Boardman?" he asked.

Ellen reached out and laid her slim hand on his. She took pride in remembering what the heavier, stronger, now badly bruised hands had done for her.

The door opened and Linda came in, walking briskly and rubbing a towel behind her ears. Virgil glanced at Ellen to see how she would take Linda's nudity, and read no reaction at all.

"Virgil!" Linda stopped and looked at him, and he was afraid of what she might say. "Why can't all men be like you?"

In his whole lifetime no one had ever said such a thing to him before. He dropped his head as his throat went tight and dry. He forgot the attractive girl who stood nude before him; he forgot the others who were there, and remembered only that in one fleeting fragment of time he had been judged as a man and had not been found wanting.

He was for those few seconds no longer a Negro: he was

not of any race; he was simply a human being who had managed to do something well.

It was one of the greatest moments of his life. He looked at his sore hands, relaxed, and then came back to earth.

"Thank you," he said, and hoped she would understand.

Emily did. "Why don't you get dressed," she said to her daughter, "so we won't keep Virgil waiting too long?"

Linda shook her blond head. "I can be ready in two minutes," she exaggerated. "But if Virgil is going to tell us how he found out, and how he learned what he knew, I don't want to miss a word."

"Please," Ellen said.

Carole arrived at the table with a cup of coffee and one of Emily's home-baked sweet rolls. "Would you rather have iced tea?" she asked.

Virgil wanted very much to say yes, but remembered that the coffee was already poured and that he was a guest. He hesitated for only a moment, and Carole, with the perception of an adult, ran for the refrigerator. Linda hurried from the room.

"I'm sorry we don't have any cold beer to offer you," Forrest apologized. "Unfortunately it's taboo in nudist parks."

"Iced tea would be wonderful," Tibbs answered.

The iced tea was provided. Virgil added lemon and sugar, stirred, and drank deeply. He was content just to sit with these agreeable people and enjoy one of the few periods of true relaxation he had known in many days.

In a short time Linda was back, dressed and with a hairbrush in her hand. "O.K.," she said, and sat down to listen.

Virgil found that everyone was looking at him.

"I promised you an explanation because you are entitled to one," he began, "but I'm afraid it won't be very dramatic."

Forrest spoke to his younger daughter. "Carole, this won't be very interesting for you, so you can go down to the playground if you would like."

"Must I?" Carole asked.

"I think it would be a good idea."

Clearly disappointed, Carole slid off her chair and exited through the doorway to the big lawn. When she was gone, Forrest looked at Tibbs once more and indicated that he should go on.

"You all know the start," Virgil said. "The body of the late Dr. Roussel was found in your pool entirely stripped except for a set of contact lenses. That looked like a promising clue, but when I ran the lenses down, they led straight up a blind alley. After Miss Boardman mentioned her uncle's absence, an alert police officer picked it up and we had our first break."

"Please call me Ellen."

"Good, I'd like to. To continue, as soon as the identification was positive, several things became apparent, or appeared to do so. One of them was the fact that the death of Dr. Roussel—if you will forgive me, Ellen—seemed to be directly connected with the affairs of his holding company, as indeed it was. This focused our attention on the four surviving stockholders; normally murder takes a pretty strong motive, and a large sum of money comes under that heading."

"Not to everyone," Linda interjected.

"True, but of course everyone doesn't commit murder. All we had to go on at this point, other than what I've already told you, was the fact that the body was placed here in the pool to attract attention—in other words, so that it would be widely reported in the papers. That was a guess, but it was the only thing we could think of that fitted the facts."

"Was that actually so?" Forrest asked.

"Only in part. Right from the beginning there was a major problem and it stopped us for a long time. In this section of the country it would have been much safer to get rid of the body down one of the wild canyons in the mountains; putting it into your pool was far more dangerous, so there had to be a reason. And then where were the clothes and other personal effects?"

"I can think of one thing," Emily contributed. "And Linda has mentioned it, too. As you must know, Virgil, there are still a lot of people who can't stand the idea of nudist parks because it runs against their own prejudices. Maybe somebody wanted to get at us and took that horrible way of doing it."

"No," Tibbs answered. "Your logic is fine, but there are *two* possibilities here and you are only considering one of them."

"What's the other?" Linda demanded.

Tibbs paused a moment. "You wanted to be a detective and you started out well," he replied. "Now, see if you can figure it out. You'll have a few minutes before we come to that part."

He took another drink from his iced tea.

"The next important item," he continued, "came from a well-known source—Shakespeare."

"William Shakespeare?" George inquired, smiling.

Virgil nodded. "Do you remember in *Macbeth* the moment when the news is brought of the king's death? Instead of being shocked and grieved by the news, Lady Macbeth said,

'What, in our house?'—and gave herself away right there."

Ellen said, " 'Look to the lady:—

" 'And when we have our naked frailties hid,

" 'That suffer in exposure, let us meet,

" 'And question this most bloody piece of work.' "

Tibbs looked at her with admiration.

"I played in it once—in college," she explained. "Please go on."

"As part of the routine investigation, I called on Mrs. Pratt —as it happened, at a time when the news of Dr. Roussel's death was not yet out. That is, the identification of the body found on your premises had not been made public. When I informed Mrs. Pratt that her long-time friend and claimed fiancé was dead, she said, '*Not* the body in the nudist colony!' and Lady Macbeth came into my mind. Not only that, she named the right body in the right place, which was a most unlikely thing to do, especially since Dr. Roussel's arrival in this country had not been announced.

"Naturally that focused a good deal of my attention on that little lady. She is physically far too small to have committed the crime herself, but I was certain at that point that she had some measure of what we call 'guilty knowledge' concerning it. Either she had something to do with it directly or she knew something about it that she had no intention of revealing."

"So you pegged her on the first visit?" Holt-Rymers asked.

"Somewhat, but of course a suspicion is far from proof. Also, to be truthful with you, I didn't quite swallow her story that she and Dr. Roussel were to have been married. If she was his intended bride and was therefore in love with him, she wouldn't have described him as 'the body in the nudist colony'—the words were simply too cold and hard."

Ellen shuddered slightly, but said nothing.

"The next break came when I had a short talk with Mr. McCormack's chauffeur, Walter Brown. It was purely accidental; I didn't know that Brown existed when I went to see his employer. He was washing the car and we spoke briefly. During the course of that conversation he told me that his employer was terribly upset because a close friend of his had been killed in a nudist camp. That was a dead giveaway, since he would have no way of knowing that unless Mr. Mc-Cormack was involved and had told him, and I felt certain that wasn't so unless they both were guilty. I checked carefully and the identification had not been made public at that time."

He turned to Holt-Rymers. "Perhaps you remember telling me when I called on you that you'd just heard the news over the radio. I checked on that, and also your statement that it hadn't appeared in the morning paper. I verified your story and convinced myself that you weren't putting on an act for my benefit."

"Heaven help us sinners." The artist uncrossed his legs and crossed them the other way. "Couldn't the chauffeur have heard an earlier broadcast? I mean, aren't you cutting the time a little fine here?"

Tibbs shook his head. "Actually the news broke for the first time publicly while I was at lunch. But there is another consideration entirely that drew my serious attention to him: if he had just found out, he wouldn't have put the information so casually. There is a way we speak of things we have just learned and a very different one when we refer to things that are no longer new. He spoke in the manner of someone who has known a certain fact for some while. That was what impressed me at the time."

"In other words, he didn't tell it as fresh news," Forrest suggested.

"Exactly. In this business you have to look for things like that. Essentially there are two steps in resolving any case. First you have to find out what happened; then, after that, you have to assemble enough proof to secure a conviction in court. It isn't always the same thing. I couldn't expect to convince a jury by describing Brown's manner of speech, but for finding out what happened it was very useful."

Emily shook her head. "I don't think I would want your job, Virgil," she said.

" 'A policeman's lot is not a happy one,' " Tibbs quoted. "Now let me fit some pieces together for you. Of the four surviving stockholders in the Roussel Rights Company, two were well established financially and the other two were in desperate, or near-desperate, circumstances. Walter McCormack was clearly secure, but I checked his rating just the same. I also checked up on your statement, Bill, concerning the number of pictures you sold and the price they netted to you."

"I don't think I want to know you any more," Holt-Rymers said. "You're too dangerous to have around."

Tibbs smiled a little grimly. "Not if you're telling the truth," he said. "And you were. In a murder case you can't afford to take anything for granted. Which brings us to Mr. Peterson, the broker. Unfortunately for him, he was in a jam all the way around. He had lost most of his clients through giving them bad advice and his business was in serious trouble.

In addition, he'd had an affair with his secretary, and when she told him that she was pregnant, he panicked. He gave her a partial settlement out of what he had left and then hurried off to Europe to see Dr. Roussel."

"Why *do* people get so mixed up?" Emily asked.

"They do, all the time," Virgil said. "At least they keep policemen from being unemployed."

"He went to Europe, then, to try and dispose of his stock?" Ellen asked.

"More or less. According to the terms of the agreement among the partners, none of them could sell without common consent. However, Peterson hoped that Dr. Roussel, being a bachelor and living in Europe, might be sympathetic about his situation. He knew he would have no chance with Walter McCormack, but he thought that Dr. Roussel might be willing to advance him a substantial sum against the sale of the company—something he strongly advised."

"And badly," Holt-Rymers added.

"Is he married?" Linda asked.

"Yes, but his wife is suing him for divorce."

"Then there was only one thing for him to do: let his wife divorce him in Reno and marry the girl he got into trouble," she said.

Tibbs looked at her and shook his head. "Marrying under those circumstances seldom solves anything, particularly if you consider marriage as something more than a legal convenience. Anyway he couldn't. She was already married—to a serviceman overseas."

"Good night!" Forrest said.

"Agreed," Virgil went on. "And when you add all of these things together, you can see why Peterson might have been in a frame of mind to attempt murder. He had motive and he is a big, powerful man, which made him a definite possibility. However, from the strictly legal standpoint all he had done that was unlawful was to have an affair with a consenting adult. He had plenty to worry about, but from a police point of view he wasn't in very deep. Also if the company had been sold, most of his difficulties would have been solved for him."

"How about the girl?" Linda asked.

"She went down to Mexico for a vacation. While there, she had a slight accident and lost her child. Enough about Oswald Peterson. Now, on to Mrs. Pratt."

"No, thank you," Holt-Rymers muttered.

"Quiet," Linda retorted.

Virgil sipped his iced tea.

"Mrs. Pratt is a woman of insane vanity; her whole history proves it. Originally she turned down Dr. Roussel because at that time he couldn't provide her with enough money. Then she married an older man who could. She was diminutive and 'cute,' so that to certain men she was very appealing; she cashed that asset like a traveler's check. When she was widowed, she was left in very comfortable circumstances— enough to keep her well for the rest of her life. But that wasn't enough for her, so she planned to remarry—and again to the highest bidder. To accomplish this she bought herself a very expensive and costly-to-maintain home and worked her way into society. If she could find herself a new husband in ample circumstances, fine; if not, she was sure that Albert Roussel still desired her and he was now making lots of money."

"She should have grabbed him," George commented.

"Don't wish that on Uncle Albert," Ellen said a little tartly.

"Sorry," George apologized.

Virgil continued, "She splurged far beyond her income and didn't receive the romantic returns she expected. She was certainly no longer young and some of her less desirable traits of character were beginning to show through. So when her money began to run out, she wrote to Dr. Roussel and more or less put herself on the block. He turned her down.

"Hurrah!" Ellen said. "One question—how did you find this out?"

"I had quite an extended telephone conversation with her maid. Normally I don't believe she would have told me this, even if I had asked her officially. But there was a small incident: Mrs. Pratt embarrassed her when she made tea for me during my first visit. Also she was told that I was not to be considered a guest in the house, either because of my profession or, more likely, my race. This did not set well with that young lady, so when the subject came up in our little talk, she told me about it. Of course Mrs. Pratt has very few secrets from her maid, who lives in."

"I would think not," Emily agreed.

"Now come the beginnings of murder," Virgil continued. "She was a woman scorned. This was her prime and basic motivation; to a person of her vanity, having her supposed long-time suitor refuse her hand when it was freely offered was insufferable. It was a gross humiliation and her overdeveloped ego demanded revenge."

"Hell has no fury like a woman scorned," Linda said.

"Perhaps that would not have driven her all the way to murder," Tibbs went on, "but other things piled up. She was well aware that her appeal to men as a prospective bride was all but gone. She was desperate for more money. And, despite the fact that Albert Roussel had declined to marry her, she was still firmly convinced she was his heir, at least in part. When the company was organized, he was grateful for her support and told her that she would never lose by backing him. He offered to put up what assets he had at the time. She suggested to him that a legacy might be more appropriate, just in case something happened to him. This information came to me from his lawyer, who convinced him not to follow that suggestion."

"I understood that a client's conversations with his attorney were privileged," Forrest said, making it a question.

"That's correct," Tibbs agreed. "But this was not the same thing. In this case the client had been murdered and I appealed to Mr. Wolfram to help me bring the persons responsible to justice. He was not required to answer me, but he chose to do so."

"I see," Forrest acknowledged. "One more thing, Virgil: do people ordinarily go to the extreme of murder just for revenge? In Italian operas, yes, but I find it hard to believe."

"That's because you're a decent and well-adjusted person," Virgil answered him. "But how many times have you picked up a newspaper and seen something that began with the words 'estranged husband'? Unfortunately it's a too familiar pattern. A husband and wife break up; after the separation the woman starts seeing another man. The estranged husband bursts in on them, does some shooting, and often ends up by killing himself."

"Of course!" Linda interjected.

"As far as money went, she still owned the stock," George pointed out.

"Yes, she did. But she couldn't sell it. Dr. Roussel opposed the sale of the company and had told her so."

"I'm beginning to see," Emily said. "With Dr. Roussel out of the way, she might be able to force the sale. She probably knew about Peterson and his troubles."

"That's right."

"Wait a minute," Ellen said. "Suppose she believed that the money in the estate would go to Mother—that is, the cash and assets like that—but that Uncle Albert would have left her the stock for what she did for him. It would be very logical. In that case she could force the sale and take in twice as much."

Tibbs nodded slowly. "I had the same thought. I can't prove it's right—not without a confession—but I'm sure of it just the same."

Linda took over. "She knew McCormack's chauffeur and got him—somehow—to do her dirty work for her."

"That's a little too fast," Tibbs said. "Basically you're right, but it isn't that simple. It begins with the fact that Brown at one time was a decent enough man. He worked for Mr. McCormack for a considerable time. I learned that when he described the late Mrs. McCormack to me and said that she had died some time before. He was much better off than he realized; despite a limited education he had steady employment, a comfortable place on the estate to live, and, like all the members of Mr. McCormack's household, he had been generously remembered in his employer's will. He was to have received a legacy of two thousand dollars for each year of continuous service, which is a lot more than most people are able to save. He didn't know that, but he should have realized that since his employer had no visible heirs, he would very likely be liberal toward those who had served him faithfully. But he didn't reason this out and I guess McCormack's attitude toward his staff was not encouraging."

"Do you know what got him off the track?" Forrest asked.

Tibbs hesitated. "Unfortunately I do. Part of it is due to the fact that he is a Negro and part of it is due directly to the scheming of Mrs. Pratt. Like myself, Brown came originally from the Deep South and his people are still down there. When the racial demonstrations first hit the place where he had lived, his only sister took an active part in a local biracial committee which was working toward peaceful equality—that is, until she was seized by some local white degenerates and raped. When Brown learned of this, he promptly joined one of the most militant of the Negro radical groups, and within a short time he built up a considerable hatred of Caucasians. He went so far as to take the club's full course in street fighting—and, believe me, it's a good one."

Virgil shook his head; when he went on, his voice was in a lower key, and flatter. He was simply reciting facts.

"Mrs. Pratt knew Brown because Mr. McCormack, who is handicapped, seldom leaves his home and he frequently sent his car for her when there was business to discuss."

"I can verify that," Holt-Rymers contributed.

"Once or twice Brown had invited out Mrs. Pratt's maid, who is a most respectable young lady. In telling me about it she informed me that Brown was among those arrested in the Watts riots which took place in the summer of 1965 in Los Angeles. She learned of it through a Negro newspaper; when she saw Brown's name and photograph, she told her mistress about it to caution her. That's what actually started things off."

Virgil stopped and finished his iced tea. Linda promptly refilled his glass and then looked at him with lifted eyebrows.

"Knowing what she did about Brown, Mrs. Pratt dealt one off the bottom of the deck," he said. "She told him that her people had once lived in the South and that she herself was one-sixteenth Negro—which, thank heavens for my people, was a lie—and that when she had told Dr. Roussel of this, he had broken their engagement and refused to marry her."

"Of all things!" Linda exploded.

Tibbs drank some tea and continued. "When she had Brown thoroughly enraged at this supposed insult, she offered him a substantial sum of money to arrange some sort of 'accident.' Each time Dr. Roussel had visited the States in recent years, Mr. McCormack had sent his car to the airport to meet him, since they were very close friends. She gave Brown five hundred dollars in advance, by check, and wrote on it 'for landscaping.'

"Wasn't that plain stupid?" George asked.

"Of course it was, but she had the idea that when the check came back from the bank, she would be able to hold it over Brown's head forever. She didn't know, or had forgotten, that all checks which go through the clearinghouse are photographed. Anyway, I saw it before it was returned to her. It surprised me very much, so I got in touch with the gardeners' association and found out who takes care of her place. I have a statement from him that no one else has worked on the property for some time.

"I'll make the rest brief, if I may. Brown's recent hatred of Caucasians, which was prejudice in direct reverse, was inflamed by the Watts affair and fanned even more by his belief that Dr. Roussel had refused to marry Mrs. Pratt because of her supposed Negro blood. He was well trained in violence and ready to act. Then Mrs. Pratt pushed him even farther,

and it was her undoing. I have explained that she was a woman scorned—a vicious, arrogantly egotistical, totally undisciplined, and spiteful woman—who wanted revenge and demanded it in spades. When the Western Sunbathing Association held its annual convention here, you got a great deal of
publicity, as you know. That gave Mrs. Pratt her idea. She
not only wanted Dr. Roussel killed; she wanted his body
specifically left on your grounds."

A look of comprehension came over Linda's face. "The
other possibility!" she exclaimed. "It wasn't to embarrass *us;*
it was to reflect on *him!*"

"Yes, but it took me quite some time to figure that one out.
Brown went along with it because he thought that in a nudist
resort any unwanted bodies would be disposed of without a
word said. He supposed that you lived on the wrong side of
the law."

Forrest slowly shook his head. "That's one of the things
Comstock did to this country," he said quietly.

George had been thinking. "The body being nude, it took
a lot longer to identify, which probably cut down the risk.
I'll bet he got rid of the clothing and whatever luggage there
was in one of the canyons. If he'd done the same thing with
the body, we might not have found it yet."

"I agree," Tibbs said. "If we obtain a confession—and I
think we will—then we'll get Brown to show us the spot so
we can recover the evidence."

"One question more," Linda cut in. "How did he explain
Dr. Roussel's non-arrival to Mr. McCormack?"

"That's a very good point," Virgil complimented her.
"Brown had planned a simple story. He had been directed to
pick up Dr. Roussel at the airport and to drive him to his

sister's lodge in the mountains. Since the plane was due in from Europe at a very late hour, he decided to say that the doctor had hesitated to disturb his sister and her family after midnight and had asked instead to be dropped in front of a hotel in San Bernardino. Of course Brown would have been expected to obey any such instructions. He planned to say that he had done as requested—had dropped the doctor in front of the hotel and had then returned home. At that hour there would be no doorman; he was quite sure of that. It could not be held against him that there were no witnesses. Certainly it was not a very good fabrication, but its simplicity gave it some merit and it would have been very difficult to disprove. He would be interrogated very closely, but he'd had experience with the law and he was confident that nothing could be proved against him."

"Lie detector?" Holt-Rymers asked.

"The subject has to volunteer and the evidence obtained can't be admitted in court if it tends to establish guilt. Which is something to remember: if you are ever wrongly accused of a crime, ask at once for a polygraph test. Most police departments have one. We do. A suspect who does this is almost always innocent. If the machine establishes that he is speaking the truth, then for all practical purposes his worries are over."

"Thank you. That's useful to know. But go on."

"As it worked out, Brown never told his story. The flight was delayed and came in after Mr. McCormack had retired. Brown took the call from the airport and, as instructed, went down. After his return he had the car refilled with gas, put it away, and was never asked for an explanation. I suppose McCormack thought Dr. Roussel was at his sister's. Brown debated telling his employer that he had picked up Dr. Roussel, but since he seemed to have got an unexpectedly good break, he decided to say nothing. He could always claim later that he had assumed Mr. McCormack knew. He sensed his proposed explanation was a little thin, and not having to use it seemed a good deal safer. In that he was right."

Ellen sat still, her hands in her lap. She was quiet for a long time; then she sighed and looked up.

"Thank you—Virgil," she said.

"You're very welcome," he answered. "It was only my job."

In a few minutes the atmosphere began to clear. The dark shadows of murder yielded to the intense California sunlight that seemed almost to be burning sharp designs through the windowpanes and onto the floor. The singing of birds penetrated into the kitchen and Carole, somehow aware that she was now permitted, slipped quietly back into the room.

Ellen stood up and looked down at the others. "You've all been a comfort," she said. Bill Holt-Rymers, who had been watching her for some time, grinned and then made an announcement.

"I shall paint you," he declared in a voice that allowed of no discussion.

Ellen glanced at the portrait of Linda and hesitated. "Can you do pictures—with clothes on?" she asked.

"I can," Holt-Rymers replied. "But my heart isn't in it. Still—"

Virgil glanced at his watch. "Since we have an appointment with Captain Lindholm—" he began.

"I'll take Ellen in my car," George volunteered. "You'll have a full load."

"I'm staying, if you don't mind," Holt-Rymers said as he

rose to his feet. "I'm getting allergic to clothes on hot days, and I have work to do."

He walked to the easel and took down the portrait. Carrying it carefully by the edges, he handed it to Virgil. "Yours," he said.

"I can't accept—" Tibbs began.

"Yes, you can. This time I got the drop on you. I phoned Chief Addis, and he approved. Your picture, as a token of my appreciation."

Virgil took the valuable canvas between his hands and looked at it unbelievingly.

"It's not an accident," Linda said. "We wanted you to have it. I sat for it and Bill painted it. Of course what he did was far more than I could do, but it's for you anyway."

"I . . ." Virgil Tibbs ran out of words.

"It might look quite nice in your office," Holt-Rymers suggested. His face gave no clue as to whether he was serious or not.

Virgil assumed that he was. "It's to your credit that you don't know much about police stations," he said. "At the office I'm supposed to get some work done. With this wonderful picture on the wall, I'd have no privacy. If it's really mine, then please may I put it in my apartment."

"Then it's for your apartment. You pay for the frame. Cheers."

Carrying the exquisite portrait, Virgil walked with the Nunns to the parking lot. He put Emily and Linda in the back of the official car and entrusted the picture to their care. Then he assigned Carole to the middle of the front seat and asked Forrest to sit on the right. George took Ellen in his own car and prepared to follow.

Tibbs started the engine, drove out of the grounds, and turned westward toward Pasadena. "This won't be an ordeal," he assured his guests. "There will be a few formalities and that's all."

"I want to ask something," Forrest said from across the seat. "Now that Ellen isn't here, why was an attempt made on her life? It doesn't make sense to me."

Virgil glanced in the mirror and saw that George and Ellen were following at a safe distance. "Because she was due to inherit the estate Mrs. Pratt was after. Brown learned all about it when he drove Mr. McCormack out to see her. If something happened to Ellen before she formally inherited, then Mrs. Pratt saw herself as next in line. Her vanity is such that she couldn't believe Dr. Roussel wouldn't remember her generously, and affectionately.

"As for Brown," Virgil said, "he wanted the money he had been promised, and what he thought was revenge against the whites who had insulted his people. So there you have it."

When they reached Highway 66, it amused Forrest to note how the motorists suddenly went on their good behavior as soon as they saw the police car. Virgil drove calmly, largely in the right-hand lane, and stayed carefully within the shifting speed limits. Soon he and Forrest dropped into a conversation about the final third of the baseball season, and Carole became excessively bored. In the back seat Emily and Linda rode in silence, the painting on the seat between them. The thing was over now, but the shadows it had cast refused to go away entirely. Emily looked out the window and lost herself in thought.

They passed Santa Anita, moved along the foothills, and crossed Sierra Madre Villa. Then Virgil picked up the micro-

phone, spoke with it close to his lips, and after a moment replaced it in the clip.

Reaching under the dashboard, he flipped a switch; a red
light on the panel went on. In the light traffic he picked up
speed until the car was doing a little under forty. Then he hit
the siren.

Carole came immediately and fully to life. Ramrod straight
she sat up in the seat, her eyes aglow. "Are the red lights on?"
she demanded.

"They are," Tibbs answered. "When I make a promise, I
keep it."

"Oh, golly!" Carole cried.

"With permission," Virgil answered, largely for her father's
benefit.

A red traffic light loomed ahead. The commanding voice of
the siren held traffic motionless while Tibbs expertly cut to
the left around the stopped cars and then pulled back onto the
right side. In full Code 3 condition the police car moved
down Colorado Boulevard.

Linda leaned forward and looked at her little sister's glowing face. "Can we do this again sometime?" Carole asked.

"The next time you help me catch a murderer," Virgil answered her.

"I'll try," she promised eagerly.

For her the shock of all that had happened was over.

Virgil smiled a little grimly. With sharp professional skill
he swung around a minor street excavation, straightened out
the car once more, and headed down the famous street into
the center of the city he called home.

Format by Katharine Sitterly
Set in Linotype Janson
Composed and printed by York Composition Company, Inc.
Bound by The Haddon Craftsmen, Inc.
HARPER & ROW, PUBLISHERS, INCORPORATED